She had become his prey. His plaything. The one he desired the most, but someone wanted her more.

Her resilience fading, Rebecca fights to remain strong against the man trying to destroy her mind and her life. Without the solace of Eric's arms, Rebecca's will to recover from the relentless blows wanes as she begins to break.

Eric, forced to face his own choices, races to end the nightmare before the woman he loves is completely torn apart.

Just when they think the worst is over, the game and the stakes change.

This book is a work of fiction. Names, characters, places, and incidents either are products of the author's imagination or are used fictitiously. Any resemblance to actual events or locales or persons, living or dead, is entirely coincidental.

Veiled Deception
Copyright © 2019 Amy Romine
ISBN: 978-1-4874-2466-4
Cover art by Martine Jardin

Published by eXtasy Books Inc or
Devine Destinies, an imprint of eXtasy Books Inc

Look for us online at:
www.eXtasybooks.com or www.devinedestinies.com

Veiled Deception
Trust Me, Book 2

By

Amy Romine

DEDICATION

My husband, Robert, our three children and my extended family. To Brenda (my Donna), Sean, the man with the knowledge, and finally my professional family whose constant support will never be forgotten.

CHAPTER ONE

Eric sat through a barrage of unneeded attention for a simple flesh wound. After what seemed like forever, the doctors released him. It was early evening when Eric stepped onto the sidewalk. He saw several messages waiting for him and he began to listen to them when Adam pulled up with the car.

He got in and his phone buzzed. He lifted it, seeing Charlie's name.

"Hey, what's up?"

"Are you on your way?"

"On my way where?"

"Rebecca's house."

"What? Why are you at . . ."

"Eric, it's . . . it's bad."

Eric's heart dropped. Breathless, he looked to Adam.

"I got her out, but she won't stop shaking. She won't talk or look at me. It's like she's in a trance . . ."

"What happened?" Eric felt the car accelerate and Adam turned on the emergency lights.

"Someone broke into her house and covered it . . . Everything is covered in . . . blood . . ." Charlie started, his words broken and hesitant.

Eric's mind went to the buckets of blood.

"I've never seen anything like it, whoever did this . . ."

"Did you already call the police?"

"Yeah, but they aren't here yet."

"Okay, Charlie, you need to listen to me." He tried to stay

focused and compartmentalize the images rushing at him. "Rebecca's going into shock. Put her in the car and turn on the heat. You need to keep her calm and warm until the police arrive."

"How far out are you?"

"About half an hour, we'll get there as soon as we can," Eric replied before he hung up the phone.

"Black and Whites will be on scene in less than five minutes," Adam told him. "I called Misty, Lug and a bus. How bad is it?"

"I . . . it sounds . . . bad."

They pulled up alongside three patrol cars parked in front of the house. Jogging to the front door, a uniformed officer burst out of the house. Eric looked to Adam in confusion and the officer proceeded to vomit into the bushes. They stepped across the threshold, seeing pairs of flat foots covering their mouths, standing in awe of the view.

His memory of her house was full of light, comfortable and warm. A chill ran up his back and his stomach lurched in revulsion. Surrounded by dripping crimson and the suffocating odor of iron, the walls were covered in a thick coat of blood.

Eric didn't remember what color the couch was before, but it was now a deep soaked purple with blood dripping down the sides. Two more officers exited the house and he forced himself to remain steady against the revolting display.

"Where's Misty?"

"She just pulled up." Adam stepped out of the house to get their expert.

Beccs . . .

He tried not to think of Rebecca walking into the house and seeing this for the first time, but there was no way to avoid it. He could almost envision how it happened and his entire body tensed in rage.

"Wow," he heard a female voice say and saw Misty walk into the house. "This is some seriously fucked up shit."

"Get to work. I want this bastard rotting in a jail cell sooner rather than later."

Eric looked to Adam, who nodded in acknowledgement. He stepped out of the house and searched for Charlie. He found him just beyond the driveway talking to Lugow. Eric moved to his brother's side, his chest quaking in dread. "Charlie."

"Eric, how . . ."

"Try and not to think about it, Charlie, it won't help anything," Lug offered.

"Yeah."

"Is Rebecca in the car?" Eric asked.

"Yeah."

Eric saw her through the window.

"I did everything you said. Lugow tried to talk to her, but . . ."

"I managed to get her to take couple sips of water, but that's about it," Lugow replied, giving him a look of genuine concern.

Eric's chest tightened even more.

"Addison said there's a pile up downtown. All the ambulances are tied up so they have no idea when they'll get here."

"Do you mind if I try and talk to her?" Eric asked and Lugow nodded his okay. Eric gave his brother a pat on the back and moved around to the passenger's side of the car. He reached for the handle of the door. He pulled on it, trying not to startle her.

The door opened and despite his efforts, she jumped back in confusion and fear. She saw him and blinked. Her entire body trembled and her arms wrapped around themselves.

Eric pulled off his jacket, bundling it around her thin body. "Beccs." He pulled the jacket tight, before he touched her chin. "Rebecca, can you look at me?"

There was no doubt, she was in shock. The trauma of finding her home violated to such an extreme manner would send anyone cowering in disbelief. She met his gaze, her eyes wide and distant.

"Hey, bright eyes." His thumb caressed her cheek and her eyes closed at his touch. She trembled again and it took every ounce of strength not to enclose himself around her and take her away. He knew better and pulled himself back into the real world.

"Charlie's going to take you somewhere safe, where you can rest." She stared up at him blankly. He decided not to give her a choice of accommodations. He wanted her where he could keep an eye on her.

His free hand rested on the edge of the seat and he felt her icy hand grasp it, her eyes dipping when her breath stuttered in her chest.

"Hey, hey," Eric responded, holding her hand between his in reassurance. "It's going to be okay. Charlie isn't going to leave you. You'll be safe."

Her eyes softened a little, but she couldn't hide the fear and pain still residing behind them. Her grip on his hand tightened.

"I'll be there as soon as I can," he said while she kept his unfaltering gaze. "I promise."

Charlie approached the door.

Eric shifted and released her hand. He glanced at his brother, seeing she'd resumed her focus on the world outside the windshield. Eric moved out of the car. His heart ached with every inch he moved, but he closed the passenger door and met Charlie.

"How is she?"

"The same."

"Can I get her out of here?"

"Yeah, hang on." He moved past Charlie to Lugow. "Do you have any problems with Charlie getting her out of here? I am going to have him take her to my dad's. She'll be safe there."

"Yeah, no get her out of here so she can rest. We can talk to her tomorrow," Lug replied.

Eric walked back to Charlie. "Lug said it is fine. Why don't you take her to Dad's for the night?"

"Dad's?"

"Yes, Dad's," Eric replied in an even tone. "She needs to rest and with both you and Dad around, she should be able to relax. This guy is still out there and Dad's house is more secure than your place, no offense."

"None taken," Charlie replied, looking to the car in concern. "Did she say anything to you?"

"No," Eric replied, he wasn't technically lying to his brother.

"She hasn't said anything since . . ."

"Charlie, she's in shock," Eric explained again in reassurance. "She needs to stay warm and relaxed. Besides that, just be there. She'll come around. She needs to process what's happened."

"Okay," Charlie replied with a nod. "You coming to the house after all this?"

"Yeah, after we're done here." His stomach twisted. Charlie nodded and moments later, Eric watched the car pull onto the street and disappear into the darkness.

The buzz around the station was filled with stories from the *bloody house*. The descriptions ranged from oozing entrails to blood dripping from the ceiling to a wading pool of it in the middle of the living room. Eric did his best to ignore the chatter, although he swore he worked in a freakin' hen house instead of a police station and focused on finding the creep.

He, Adam, Lug and Lug's team had been in the thick of it since the event. Who knew what else this idiot had planned? With no way to anticipate what this guy was going to do to try and get to her, the one thing they could do was try to catch him before he made his next move. He realized things weren't going to get better. They were going to get worse and a feeling of dread washed over him.

Around midnight his phone rang and he picked it up, seeing Charlie's name. "This is Eric," he said into the phone, his mind panicking.

"Hey, bro, I need to go to the bar."

"What happened is everything okay?"

"Yeah, the gaming inspector decided to show up and they are waiting for me."

"Sucks." He eased back into his chair, able to take a breath. "Is Dad not there?"

"He's here and Beccs asleep. I'd feel better if I knew you were here with her as well."

"Ah yeah, I'll head over."

"I need to leave now. Do you think they'll be okay here alone for a little while?"

"Yeah, if Beccs is asleep, they'll be fine. Take off, I'm on my way. "

"Okay, thanks."

I'd feel better if I knew you were here as well . . .

The torment of the situation was suffocating and yet he could see no way out. His chest tightened and he shifted his focus. He went to tell Lug and Adam he was going to sit with Beccs. They asked him to call and let them know how she was and they would see him in the morning.

According to Charlie, Rebecca was asleep, which he hoped was true. Although he knew from experience, sleep was fitful and fleeting at best. The fear he'd seen in her eyes rocked him again and his foot pushed a little harder on the gas.

Charlie loves her . . .

He'd reminded himself of this fact, but he just wasn't able to let her go. When he thought he had a handle on the situation, he found himself swept into her eyes and all sense of reason fell away. The need to be close to her had turned into almost a hunger and the longer he went, the weaker he became.

The house was dark and quiet. He parked the truck and headed to the door, thinking of the bottle of scotch in the cabinet next to the fridge. Eric pushed his key into the deadbolt, turned the doorknob and walked in the door. He caught a flash of dark red to his right and turned toward it. Rebecca was sitting alone in the window seat.

"Hey." He took in her pale face and his heart leapt in concern. "What are you doing out here all alone?"

She released a shaken breath and pushed herself deeper into the corner of the window.

He realized what was happening. She hadn't known it was him and he scared her. It wouldn't have normally had any kind of effect, perhaps a brief flash of hesitation, but given her current condition, it paralyzed her.

"You're supposed to be asleep," he said in a quiet gentle tone. He inched toward her and she buried herself in his leather jacket. She hid her face in her arms and he saw she was trembling. He reached her and crouched down, his hands at her feet. She needed time to come back from the adrenaline rush he'd spawned.

"We call them aftershocks. When someone experiences a traumatic event, shock can sometimes set in. It's the mind's way of coping with the event." He leaned on his leg and then shifted to a seat on the floor, his back against the bottom of the seat. "Aftershocks are just the way they sound.

Bursts of adrenaline brought on by a similar or equally threatening situation. Unfortunately the unfamiliar surroundings and my entrance caused this little tremor. The good news is, just like the aftershocks of an earthquake, they're usually intense, but quick to pass.

"Charlie told me you were asleep. I didn't think I would scare you Beccs. I'm sorry," he felt like a babbling idiot and after a few moments of quiet, glanced up to the window. Her tired, but now calm eyes looked back at him and he couldn't suppress the smile of relief spreading across his face.

"Better?" He rose off the floor and her eyes followed his movement. "The floor is hard and that window has to be the draftiest place in the house. How about we make a happy medium and settle on the couch?"

She lifted her head a little higher, uncurled her legs and moved to get off the seat. She got to her feet and began to wobble.

As she tried to retain her balance, Eric realized she wasn't going to recover. He caught her in his arms and found himself once again staring down into the liquid blue of her eyes. Her tiny form leaned against him and without thinking, he pulled her closer.

"I've got you." Her knees collapsed again and he kept her firmly within his arms. "Let's get you to the couch."

He eased her down and she leaned back, curling her legs beneath her. She watched him intently. He grabbed the blanket off the chair, laying it over her legs before taking the seat next to her.

Eric sat close enough to feel her warmth, but left enough space for her to feel comfortable. At this moment, he was a stranger to her and he found himself longing to see the fire in her eyes again. She rested her head against the back of the couch and he leaned back, her gaze still on him. He turned on the television for a needed distraction and began to flip through the channels. His mind was fleeting and numb and he needed his heart to stop pounding so he could think.

"I'm going to get something to drink." He rested the remote next to her. "Do you want something?"

She didn't respond and he smiled at her before rising from the couch. He could see her from the window wall, between the kitchen and the living room. He pulled a water out of the fridge and leaned against the counter, trying to clear his head.

He was willing to admit he was worried about her. He'd hoped she would've slept and allowed herself to recover from the trauma. Sleep unfortunately wasn't going to happen unless he could get her to relax. His abrupt entrance hadn't helped the situation, but there was no way to change it now. He had to do whatever she needed to get her strong enough to come back. He moved into the living room and retook his seat next to her.

"So what did we decide on?" He looked at the TV and she remained motionless on the couch beside him. The commercials ended and he saw the familiar beginning of Tom & Jerry. He remembered her mentioning it on the phone. "Nice choice, Beccs."

He saw what looked like the edge of a smile on her lips and he sat back and enjoyed the show. About an hour in, he saw her eyes begin to close. A few minutes later, she shifted and her head laid against his shoulder in slumber. Not wanting to wake her, he tried not to move, stayed where he was and let her sleep.

He was conscious to remain relaxed, in fear of the smallest jarring, even subliminal, would wake her needed slumber. Eric continued to flip through the channels and saw a documentary on the Gaza Strip. He realized it would've been a perfect distraction and it pushed his mind back to their conversation at the coffee house in Dallas. He remembered the way she laughed and smiled during their banter about their common interest. His heart ached and warmed in the same breath at the memory.

He wanted the moment back, it had been so simple. They were two people with no past and no future. The common fascination for a faraway place between them. He wanted it again. He wanted to sit with her and laugh and talk and challenge. He wanted the ease of conversation, with no pretense, no conflict and no restrictions.

He growled and scolded himself for being so selfish. He wasn't good for her, he wasn't what she needed and he could never be what she deserved.

He felt her tremble against him.

"No!" she screamed, bolting forward, her eyes wide.

"Beccs, you're okay."

She turned, her expression frozen in a confused fear.

Eric's hand went to her cheek and then brushed through her hair. She leaned into him and her head rested against his shoulder. He put his arm around her in comfort. He held her, stroking her hair, suppressing the anguish and fear in his chest. She eventually calmed and fell back to sleep.

When his eyes opened, hours later, the documentary he'd been watching was gone, replaced by an obnoxious infomercial for some ugly steam oven.

The soothing warmth surrounding him beckoned him back and his eyes closed again. Eric started to shift and realized instead of sitting on the couch, he was laying down. He could smell the sweet vanilla of her skin. His hand moved against her supple form and became entangled in her silken hair. She was nestled beneath his arm against the back of the couch and her head rested against his chest.

He allowed himself to hold her, reveling in the calm serenity pouring through him. He took a deep breath. He pushed away the overwhelming need to continue to hold her and reminded himself of the ramifications.

He needed to move.

Eric shifted and waited. She stirred, but didn't wake. He pulled himself off the couch. Her head rested on the pillow he'd just lain on before she tucked herself into his jacket and eased back into slumber. He grabbed a second blanket off the chair and covering her, found himself unable to pull his eyes away. Brushing the hair from her cheek, he placed a very soft kiss on her forehead before he forced himself to walk away.

He went to his room, pulled off his clothes and jumped in the shower. Even with the small amount of sleep, he felt good. Eric stepped into the kitchen an hour later and saw his father sitting at the table, reading the morning paper, the coffeemaker spitting in the background.

"Good morning, son," he greeted, not looking up from his paper.

"Morning." He grabbed his coffee cup and filled it before he leaned against the counter. His gaze went out to the living room and he wondered if she was still asleep.

"You look like you got about as much sleep as she did," Harry commented.

Eric redirected his eyes away. "Long night."

"Apparently," his father replied, glancing over the newspaper at him. "Charlie has his hands full at the bar, did he tell you? It was better for him to get out of here anyway. The way he was pacing around here was making me crazy and wasn't helping Rebecca relax."

"It's a lot to deal with, Dad," Eric defended, avoiding the conversation they weren't going to have. "Charlie isn't used to chaos."

"And you are?"

"Not to this extreme, but yes."

"So what happens now? Are you going to be able to catch this idiot?"

"Hopefully," Eric replied, not happy with his own response. He knew there were never any guarantees.

"Hopefully doesn't sound too promising."

"Hopefully is the best I can do for now. I need to get to the station. Are you going to . . ."

"She'll be fine. You take care of this."

"Thanks, Dad."

"Eric."

"Yeah?"

"You might want to take some Tylenol for your neck," his father commented, not looking up from his newspaper. "That couch is hard on the neck. Trust me. It's snuck up on me more than once."

Eric looked to his father, his heart thudding in his ears.

"Thanks, Dad." Eric left out the garage door to avoid disturbing Rebecca's needed slumber, but it didn't ease the pull in his chest for leaving her at all.

CHAPTER TWO

Rebecca shifted, missing the warmth that once enveloped her. She opened her eyes and found herself on a couch in a living room she didn't recognize. Thinking back, it took a minute, but she remembered Charlie bringing her to his house the previous evening, but the reason escaped her. Why was it just out of her reach? Sitting up and pushing off the blankets, she scratched her head and heard the rustling of a newspaper coming from the room behind her.

Rising from the couch, the aroma of fresh brewed coffee wafted by her and she followed it into the kitchen. Stopping at the threshold, she heard the rustling of paper again and turned to see an older man sitting at the kitchen table smiling at her.

"Well good morning."

She watched him put down the paper and rise from his chair.

"I wasn't expecting to see your pretty face for another couple hours."

She didn't say anything, but did look at the coffeepot.

He picked up on it and he moved away from the table. "Have a seat and I'll get you a cup."

She slid into the seat against the wall as he filled a cup with some coffee. "Thank you," she said with a small grin. Taking the warm cup, she filled the remainder with cream.

"You're very welcome," he replied with a nod.

She took a sip and heard the front door open.

"I'm Harry by the way. We're in here."

"Hey, there's the Phoenix herself," Charlie appeared in the doorway of the kitchen with a wide grin. "How are you feeling?"

"Much better, thanks," she replied with a small nod, still feeling a little disoriented, but at least she could think in a straight line.

Charlie sat down and started telling them the story of what happened at the bar the evening before.

While Rebecca wasn't listening, she acted like she was, allowing her mind to wander and put itself back together.

She felt vulnerable, like she was exposed with no line of defense. Her internal walls were piles of rubble and she was trying to rebuild them. The only protection she felt she had was the musk-filled leather jacket keeping her warm. She wasn't sure how it had ended up on her, but she was going to be very unwilling to give it back anytime soon.

A little while later, Harry got a phone call and Charlie announced he was going to take a shower. Rebecca refilled her cup of coffee and walked into the living room. She saw a window seat on the far wall covered in large comfortable pillows. She made her way over to it and sat down, curling her legs beneath her. She got comfortable and leaned her head against the glass, staring out the window. The sun was bright and warm and she closed her eyes, letting her mind rest for a minute, soaking it in.

"The bathroom is free if you want to get cleaned up."

Her heart jumped and she opened her eyes to look at him. "I brought your bag in from the car and put it in your room."

"Thanks."

"No problem." He leaned against the side of the couch, his hands digging into his pockets. "How much do you remember from last night?"

"Enough." She pushed her hair off her shoulder while

pulling the jacket a little tighter around her. "It's coming back in pieces."

"It'll take time, but you'll remember, unfortunately. Are you hungry? Dad doesn't usually eat until lunch, but I can make—"

"I'm fine, Charlie, thanks," she replied with a bigger smile, leaning her head back against the wall. He was obviously freaked out and she wasn't sure what to say to make him at ease so she just let him be.

A moment later, Charlie's phone rang and he pulled it out of his pocket to answer it. "Hey," he greeted. "Yeah, ah I guess . . . well if you . . . okay, we'll be down in a little while." He hung up the phone and stared at it for a moment before he met her gaze. "That was Detective Lugow. He needs us to come down to the station. He said they need to ask you some questions."

"Okay, I'll get cleaned up," she replied with a nod and moved off the seat of pillows. Her body revolted against her mental control and her limbs melted beneath her. She thought she was going to hit the floor when a strong arm wrapped around her waist, holding her upright. She looked up and met Charlie's hazel eyes, filled with a gentle deep concern. She couldn't help but feel warmed by them. "Thanks," she said trying to straighten her back within his embrace.

"You really scared me last night, Beccs."

"I'm okay, Charlie." His hand led up her back into her hair. Her cheek fell against his chest and he hugged her close to him. She allowed herself to just stop for a moment and listen to his heartbeat. It was steady and strong and she closed her eyes against it, wanting to just disappear.

Charlie's phone rang again and she took the opportunity to break their embrace. She looked to him and he nodded before she left the living room and went to search for the guest room. It only took a moment to find. Closing the door behind her, she couldn't catch her breath. She moved to the bed, lying on top of it, helpless. Curling into herself, she tried to close her eyes and recapture the warmth she'd lost.

We call them aftershocks . . . exactly the way they sound . . . the good news is, just like the aftershocks of an earthquake, they're usually intense, but quick to pass . . .

Closing her eyes again, she could see soft blue eyes staring down at her, feel his thumb touching her cheek. She clung to the image and all it brought, until her body relaxed and responded to her commands. Lifting herself off the bed, she took a deep breath, grabbed her duffel bag and headed for the shower.

"Hello, beautiful," Eric greeted, walking into Misty's lab.

"Flattery will get you nowhere, Stiles. You're too hairy for me."

"Okay then, moving on," Eric said, recovering with a smile. "What've you got for me?"

"First, I looked at the device you guys recovered in the office building downtown. There were no identifying markers, residuals or prints. I already told Lug about the contents of the package and the hair we found."

"Yeah, are you sure about the DNA match?" he asked, scratching the back of his head, his mind still a little jumbled from lack of sleep.

"Positive, I ran it three times and sent it out for independent analysis," she replied with confidence, her blonde short pony tail bouncing with her nod. "Which came back conclusive to my findings."

"Good girl, okay let's talk about the house."

"Okay, first off, wow really wow, Stiles!" Her eyes widened and she shook her head. "I'm still waiting for the results of the analysis, but I can almost guarantee the majority of the blood used is bovine."

"Cow's blood."

"Yeah, and a lot of it."

"You're sure?"

"Positive. Stiles, the human body only contains an average of 6 quarts or 5.6 liters of blood. While the average bovine carries approximately 40 liters of blood. Calculating the square-footage covered and the thickness, this guy used between seven to ten gallons of blood. The odds of him being able to obtain the amount of human blood needed to accomplish this, without someone noticing, are slim. And don't even get me started on the couch."

"Do we know if it is a match to the blood they found in the apartment?"

"Not yet, I'm working on it."

"Work faster, Mist. We need to catch this creep," Eric said with a serious smirk before he turned and exited the lab.

He leaned his head against the back of the elevator and cursed as his neck screamed at him in pain. His Dad's not so subtle comment came back to him and he couldn't help but smile. He stepped off the elevator. Adam and Lug were waiting for him. "What's up?"

"A few things actually," Lugow replied. "I got a response from Brewster, we have a sketch of our suspect. Rebecca is on her way."

Eric hesitated at the last statement, but refrained from making any kind of comment. He glanced to the right and noticed Adam watching him.

"Let's take a look," Adam suggested to Lug.

Eric forced himself to focus.

The three men collaborated behind the closed doors of one of the conference rooms.

Two hours and several discussions later, Lug excused

himself. Adam and Eric continued through the files.

"Does Charlie know how you feel about her?"

Eric hesitated, taken back by the abruptness of the comment, before he looked to his partner. He shook his head in realization. He should've known Adam would catch on .

"No, and hopefully it's going to stay that way."

"You want my advice?"

"Do I have a choice?"

"No."

Eric took a seat across from him at the table.

"Do you remember the girl I was dating when I met Olivia?"

"Allison."

"Yes, Allison," he agreed. "I was crazy for Allison, she was hot, she was sweet and she was into me. Then I go to this party. That you invited me to, by the way. I'm standing next to this amazing woman I'm nuts about, but I look across the room and I see a wisp of blonde hair, before hearing this musical laugh."

"Wait a sec ... I thought you met Olivia at Dougie's party?"

"I did, but it wasn't the first time I saw her," Adam replied with a smirk. "So for two months this woman, this mystery woman with blonde hair and a musical laugh keeps popping into my head and into my dreams. No matter what I do, I can't get her out of my head. It got so bad, I broke up with Allison and walked around like a zombie for a few weeks."

"Where was I during all of this?"

"You had your own problems to deal with, specifically psycho bitch from hell."

"Chrissy, yeah she really was a bitch wasn't she?"

"No argument. If you killed her, there wouldn't be a jury alive that would've convicted you," he said.

Eric laughed aloud.

"Okay back to my love life. So where was I?"

"Zombie."

"Yes, I was walking around like a zombie and then Dougie calls. I walked into the party, feeling like absolute dog shit. The image of this woman was still running around in my head. Then the world literally stopped. I looked up and there she was, smiling at me as she said hello. I shook her hand and the rest is history."

"Okay so that's a very sweet, romantic, story. However, I guess, I'm missing the point."

"The point is, there are no rules when it comes to the real thing," Adam explained. "One minute you're clueless and then next, your chest feels like it's going to explode if you don't see her or touch her. You're in love with her, man. I don't know what happened or how it happened, but you've fallen for this girl and there's nothing you can do to change it. You can't ignore it or deny it. When you know, you just know."

"You sound like my Dad," Eric replied, his heart feeling heavier with every passing word.

"Wise man, your dad."

"So let's say this, whatever it is, is real," Eric started, shifting in his chair. "It's not as easy as seeing her at a party and asking her on a date. First off, there's Charlie, who's totally in love with her. Then we have a stalker, slash, psychopath running around, wreaking havoc in her life. I don't think either of us can even begin to sort through any of this until some of this other crap disappears."

"I understand what you're saying, but I also know everything happens for a reason. There's a reason she walked into your life at this moment. And despite all the obstacles you laid out, it's going to play out whether you want it to or not. You just need to decide if you're ready for it."

That is the real question isn't it . . ."Wait, I thought all of this is fate."

"It is, but we always have a choice," Adam's phone rang and he stepped away from the table.

Eric sat for a moment, letting the advice settle in his gut before he rose from the table. He made is way down the hall and over to the kitchen. He popped a few quarters in the vending machine, his mind heavy in thought.

Just promise me, if you find her you won't walk away . . .

Then the world literally stopped. I looked up and there she was smiling at me as she said hello.

I wish that were true . . .

He made his way back to the conference room, two sodas in one hand. He rounded the corner and bumped into someone. He heard a gasp and turned. Her blue eyes looked at him in terror.

"Beccs."

He'd scared her again.

Damn it what is she doing out here alone?

She was breathless and he watched her body begin to quake. Her eyes watering, she looked to him, helpless. He grasped her hand and scanned his ID before he led her into an empty conference room. She propped herself against the wall and he shut the door. Her trembling worsened while tears slid down her cheeks.

He pulled her into his chest, wrapping his arms around her protectively until the trembling passed. She clung to him and he pulled her tighter against him, kissing the top of her head.

After a few minutes, she seemed to calm. He looked down at her, his hand grazing her hair. She met his gaze, her cheeks still wet with tears.

"Okay?" He gently wiped her tears away with his thumb.

A quiet desperation shone back at him and he drowned in her eyes. His heart refused to be ignored. The walls he'd so carefully built crumbled like ash. Eric leaned down, pressing his lips against hers, his hands pushing into her hair. He covered her mouth and a rush of fire swept through him. Her lips were warm and sweet. She opened up to him and he pulled her closer to him, devouring her mouth. They melted together into one enduring embrace.

He felt her pull away from him. Their lips parted and his heart screamed in protest.

"We can't do this," she said in a breathless whisper.

His forehead rested against hers, eyes closed, fighting the need to kiss her again.

"Eric . . ."

"If it was anyone else . . ." he replied with a deep growl, talking his way back from her warmth. "Rebecca, I . . ."

Her warm hand rested against his cheek and stabs of pain pushed at him like his heart was being ripped from his body. He tried to catch his breath. Her eyes were brimming with life, pain and an unquenchable warmth.

She rose up on her toes. His arms still wrapped around her, she kissed him once more. Full of emotion and regret, her lips fit within his. About to lose himself in them again, she broke away and lowered herself back to the ground. Unable to pull away from her eyes, he could see the strain and exhaustion she fought to hide. He lifted his hand, letting it graze her hair one last time, watching her close her eyes.

Like the screaming of an alarm, his cell phone rang. Her eyes opened, looking at him with strength, hiding the pain and fear only he could see. Her shoulders squared, her back stiffened and her arms dropped from his chest.

Eric kept her resilient but anguished gaze. He dropped his arms from their protective position around her. She took a step back. His cell phone rang again. She took another step and turned toward the door. He struggled with not being able to touch her or hold her. She glanced back before she opened the door. Within seconds, she had disappeared. It was a torture beyond his imagination and it was killing him.

His phone rang again and he pulled it from his pocket. "This is Detective Stiles."

CHAPTER THREE

She wasn't there.

The two guards posted outside her door were invisible because to the entire world outside her office she wasn't there.

Lugow assured her they were close to a suspect.

Close. What did that mean exactly?

The past ten days had been a rollercoaster of waiting and worrying about the other shoe and when it would drop. The nights were spent with eyes staring into the darkness. All she could see were endless flowers, dead rats, blood and a faceless woman being brutalized.

She felt cold and alone, longing to be huddled within his embrace, but the pain associated with the moment singed her again. With a last kiss, they made an unspoken agreement. They couldn't be together. Charlie was his brother and he couldn't betray him. This was a fact she'd lived with since she'd discovered he was Charlie's brother. The thing torturing her was the emotion in his eyes. The decision was killing him. She wasn't sure if the realization made the pain better or worse.

She'd been trapped in, first Donna's and now Mindy's, apartment for the past ten days. The isolation was driving herself, Mindy and her new bodyguards, nicknamed Frick and Frack, crazy. She thought coming to the office would give her something to focus on.

It didn't seem to be working.

The door of her office started to swing open. She stared at

it, gulping back the overwhelming terror continuing to grip her.

"Beccs, I have the files you asked for," Mindy said with a grin, moving into the room. "There are more . . ."

Rebecca realized she was trembling again.

"Beccs . . ."

"I'm fine, what were you saying about the files?" Rebecca snapped, her friend looking at her in confusion.

"Maybe this wasn't such a good idea. We should get you ho . . . back to the apartment."

"No!" Rebecca objected. "There is work to do here and I am not done and I'm not leaving."

"Rebecca you need to rest . . ."

"How can you have any clue as to what I need?" Rebecca snapped in weary frustration. "It's easy to say Beccs relax, or Beccs you need to sleep, or even Beccs calm down when you're not the one being tortured!"

"I understand—"

"You have no idea, Mindy! You got off lucky with a box of blood! Try seeing your entire life covered in the stuff! You're not living through this, I am! So stop acting sympathetic because I don't want it or need it!" Rebecca thrashed at her in fueled rage. "I have work to do. So either focus on the task at hand or go home and play the damsel in distress! I'll call Charlie and tell him to get his white horse ready."

She watched her friend's gaze drop before she turned and exited the office. The door closed and Rebecca collapsed in her chair. Realizing what she'd done, regret poured out of her. She rose from her chair and walked out to the office, looking for Mindy. She saw no sign of her and turned back to the office door, faced by her two companions. She glanced at them before she disappeared again behind the door.

"There's something we haven't looked into yet." Lug sat back in his chair.

"What?"

"Seattle."

"You think it's worth pursuing?" Adam asked.

Eric internally debated the point.

"I don't know, what's the likelihood of this guy stalking Rebecca as some sort of revenge for what happened with her sister?"

"It's a little extreme, don't you think?"

"I don't know, what do you think, Eric?" Lug asked.

Eric continued to chew on the ramifications of involving Lucy Gailen in the equation. "Rebecca specifically kept the details of Seattle hidden to protect Lucy," Eric started, laying the debate on the table.

"Nothing has happened to Lucy thus far."

"Maybe that's why nothing's happened."

"What?"

"Until a few weeks ago, Rebecca was the only one who knew where Lucy was. What if he isn't after Rebecca at all and he wants Lucy? What if all of this has been to try and force Rebecca into inadvertently telling him where Lucy is?"

"But why the stalking, the murders? If he wants Lucy and he knows how to get to her, why drag it all out, leaving the chance of getting caught?"

"Maybe he's stalling, waiting for something?"

"It still doesn't add up. This guy is emotional but calculating. The acts toward Rebecca and the subsequent murders are psychotic in nature, not some guy looking for his girlfriend."

"Okay let's think about this. If Rebecca pulled her out of there as quickly as she said, she didn't take anything with her, leaving all of Lucy's information behind for Marco to use. He starts tracking Rebecca from Seattle, the flowers and gifts. When he's ready, he comes to Vegas. He gets to Vegas and the stalking gets worse and we start finding bodies. He knows where Rebecca is, why not just go to the source?"

"I don't know, maybe we should ask Lucy?"

"Has Rebecca seen Lucy since she dropped her off?"

"Yeah, there was an incident a few weeks ago and she drove out there."

"Could someone have followed her?"

"I doubt it. I had a hard time following her."

"You were with her?"

"Yeah, that's how I know how to find Lucy."

Rebecca opened her bottle of water and took a sip, staring out into the navy sky. She thought of what she wanted her life to be after all of this was over and she struggled to see anything. She didn't know what she wanted. She thought she did, but things had changed and not in a good way. The life she'd built here was now filled with painful memories and piles of destruction. She wasn't one to run away, but given the circumstances, it might not be a bad idea. She could have Lucy transferred to a different hospital, one better equipped to deal with her problems, and they could both start fresh.

New town, new people, new life.

Then she thought about all of the people she'd be leaving behind, people she loved. Mindy, Donna, Charlie . . . Eric. Rebecca heard the door open and Mindy poked her head in.

"Hey," she said, her face hesitant, preparing for another lashing.

"Mindy, I . . ." Rebecca rose from her chair, her eyes tearing in regret.

"It's okay, Beccs, really." Her expression eased.

"I really didn't mean to take all of that out on you. I'm so sorry."

"Beccs, seriously, it's fine. No hard feelings," Mindy reassured, hugging her friend.

Rebecca wiped away her tears.

"Hey, I have an idea, how about I call Don and we all go out and get a drink after work?"

"That would be nice."

"Cool, I'll call her now," Mindy pulled a pile of files off her desk and walked out of the office.

Rebecca continued her battle against the mountain of paperwork and emails.

A few hours passed and Mindy would walk into the office with files she needed, or walk out with files she'd finished with. During her last exit, Rebecca heard a yawn and looking at the clock, she realized it was after seven. She leaned back in her chair and wondered what time they were supposed to meet Donna. Rebecca rose from her seat and stepped out of the office. The bullpen was deserted and quiet.

"Mindy?"

"Yeah?" She appeared from the back of the office.

"What time are we meeting Don?"

"Oh yeah, eight ... we'd better get going," Mindy said with a giggle.

Rebecca turned into the office and began packing up her stuff.

A couple minutes later, Mindy had cleared out any stragglers and they were getting ready to leave. Rebecca locked her office door, Frick and Frack stood at her side. They headed to the left when she saw the conference room light was on just down the hall.

"Someone left the light on," Rebecca moved toward the lit room. She stepped into the room and flipped the light switch. Something pulled her back and an arm cinched her waist. Rebecca tried to scream, but something covered her mouth. She fought against the hold around her arms, a rush of heat flashing through her.

"Beccs?" she heard someone call, a sickening sweet smell causing her brain to paralyze itself. She could feel herself falling and then there was blackness.

Dr. Schaffer appeared in the hallway before them and Eric moved toward him.

"Mr. Stiles, isn't it?"

"Yes, it's actually Detective Stiles, and this my partner, Detective Matheson."

"Nice to see you again. I hope there isn't a problem of some kind, is Rebecca okay?"

"Ms. Gailen is fine, but we need to speak with Lucy Gailen." Eric realized what he was about to do. He knew how protective Rebecca was of her sister. Even knowing the consequences, Eric had driven out to the hospital with the intention of interviewing Lucy without telling her

"Can I ask what this is about?"

"We really can't give you any details, just that it's in regards to a current murder investigation," Adam replied.

"Well as you know, Detective, Lucy is in a very fragile state right now and I . . ."

Eric remembered Lucy on top of Rebecca with a hypodermic needle. "I realize that, but I'm afraid we must insist." Eric held up a warrant giving them access to Lucy. *It's too late now . . .*

"Fine, fine, just follow me," Dr. Schaffer replied with a nod and they followed the man down the long hallway. "She's had to remain in isolation since the incident. I can only allow one of you in the room at a time. We have an adjoining observation area where you can watch the conversation."

Adam looked to Eric and nodded, having decided in the car if they had to interview Lucy, he should be the one to do it. Adam disappeared into the observation booth and the doctor escorted Eric into the adjoining room. They stepped toward the door and he noticed an orderly lingering at the end of the hallway

Eric heard the door open and refocused on the task at hand.

The bright room seemed inviting, but was cold and Eric found her seated in a chair beside a large picture window facing the grounds.

"Lucy, you have a visitor," the doctor said as they walked into the room and closed the door.

Eric looked to the man and he nodded the okay before Eric began to move. Coming alongside her, he pulled an empty chair out of the corner and took a seat just to the right, facing her.

"Hi, Lucy, My name is Detective Stiles. I need to ask you a couple questions about this man," Eric handed her a picture of Marco Valnes.

She took the photo and began to look it over.

"Do you recognize this man, Lucy?"

She was slender with golden hazel eyes and long, bone straight, mouse brown hair. The complete opposite of Rebecca's curls, but with familiar features.

She stared at the photo and then returned her focus to the scenery outside the window.

"Lucy, we think this man is hurting people and it might be because he's looking for you. Do you know why he's looking for you, Lucy?" He received no response. He glanced down at his hands in frustration before he noticed her hand reaching for her collar.

"Lucy, do you know why is Marco looking for you?" Eric asked and she met his eyes. He crouched down in front of her chair in desperation. "We think this man is trying to hurt Rebecca." He held the picture in front of her, hoping the reference to her sister would garner some kind of response. "I need your help to stop him from hurting her. Do you have any idea where he is, Lucy? Is there anything you can tell me about him, anything at all? Please . . ."

"Beccs, where's Beccs?" she asked him in a timid soft voice.

"Beccs is not here right now, but I know she misses you," he offered, his heart hopeful at the contact.

"No."

"Lucy, do you know this man?"

"She hates me."

"No, she doesn't. Your sister loves you," he answered, trying to pull her along. "She's trying to protect you. I need you to help me protect her. Why is Marco looking for you Lucy?"

"It's a secret," Lucy said, closing her eyes as she let out a low growl.

Eric could see her body beginning to tense.

"Momma said it was mine, not hers."

"What's a secret?" Eric asked, desperate to put the pieces together. "You can tell me, I won't tell anyone, I promise."

"Secret . . ."

"What secret, Lucy?"

"*No!*" she screamed at the top of her lungs.

He fell back against the window in shock.

"*I hate her! I hope she dies!*" She shrieked like an animal and then began to attack him.

He was able to hold her off. A moment later, the nurses arrived to try and contain her. She fought against them. They overpowered her and managed to sedate her. Eric watched her crumple into the arms of one of the male nurses. They laid her on the bed. Eric commanded his legs to move and walked out of the room, speechless.

"That was intense. Are you okay?" Adam asked, meeting him in the hall.

"Yeah I . . ." Eric started, still trying to shake it off. "I just didn't expect her to . . ."

"Yeah well I don't think a psychic could've predicted that response," Adam replied with a shake of his head. "What do you want to do now?"

"I have no idea."

The doctor exited the room.

"Hey, is she going to be okay? I didn't mean to . . ."

"It wasn't your fault, Detective. Lucy is in a very volatile state right now. There's no way to predict what's going to set her off."

"How long has she been here?"

"Rebecca checked her in about three months ago."

"What was her state when she was brought in?"

"Is Rebecca really in danger?"

"Yes, unfortunately she is," Adam, replied.

"Does your warrant cover patient information as well?"

"Yes," he said, knowing Adam would go along with the slight deception.

"Alright, come with me, I think the file is on my desk," he replied and they followed him to his office. "Here it is. All the pictures are from the day she arrived. We have to document any scars, injuries and such for insurance reasons."

Eric took the file and opened it, seeing the photos of Lucy's thin, bruised body. There were track marks on her arms, legs and with her sunken eyes and colorless cheeks, she looked like a walking skeleton. They read through the file and began to understand what they were dealing with. "You said Rebecca brought her here?"

"Yes, she called ahead, and about a day later, arrived," he replied. "She had to be present when we checked Lucy in due to the paperwork."

"Did she tell you what happened when she went to get Lucy?"

"She didn't say specifically, but she was pretty beat up when I saw her," he replied. "Wherever Lucy was, I know she didn't arrive here voluntarily. Rebecca went in and got her out."

"Did Lucy have any personal effects when she arrived that you may have put in storage?"

"Anything Lucy may have had, Rebecca took with her when she left. We don't allow patients to bring anything into the facility."

"Okay, thanks, Doc, we appreciate your help," Adam said, holding out his hand.

Eric noticed the same orderly rounding the corner away from them. He was tall, well built, shaved head and a barb-wire tattoo around his left bicep.

"Please let us know if you think of anything else that may be helpful," Adam continued. "Or if anything happens with Lucy."

"Yes of course," he agreed with a nod before he shook Eric's hand and they left.

Rebecca struggled to open her eyes and nausea swept through her like a tidal wave. She commanded her body to move, and after a few moments, managed to sit up. Her head throbbed. She looked around. She was on the floor of the conference room. She remembered she'd come to turn off the light, but everything else was blank.

She gripped the closest chair and pulled herself up. Swaying on her feet, her legs wobbled beneath her.

"Mindy?" she called out into the office. When she heard no response, she willed her body to move. She stumbled to the doorway, her vision still going in and out of focus. She took a breath and straightened her back, pushing herself to walk along the wall of the hallway. "Mindy, are you there?"

Her heart began to pound in panic when again she heard no response. She forced herself to move faster. The doorway to her office was just ahead. Her feet caught on something and she tripped and landed hard on the bullpen floor. She cursed in frustration. She lifted herself off the ground and shifted to see what it was she'd fallen over.

To her horror, she found one of her bodyguards lying unconscious beside her legs. Rebecca turned in search of the other guard and saw him unconscious a few feet away.

"Mindy!" Rebecca yelled, scrambling to her feet, her body trembling in fear. Panic filling her chest, she searched for her friend. Then she saw her open office door. She knew she'd locked it when she left and her gut clenched in agony. She stepped into the office and saw her chair turned toward the window.

She knew what was waiting for her. He body shook uncontrolled, tears streaming down her face. Her body moved without thought, propelled by the horror of anticipation. She rounded the desk and the first sliver of her friend's form appeared.

Her heart and lungs ceased to fill. She rounded the last corner and faced the chair. Her pretty friend's chocolate eyes stared at her in frozen stark fear. She was covered in blood. It began at her neck and flooded down her body. It was then Rebecca saw the blood-soaked note. Single letters cut from a magazine and pasted to a piece of white paper.

No one can protect you, Rebecca.

I'll hear you scream again.

No . . . no . . . Mindy . . . no . . .

Rebecca took several unconscious steps back and she hit the far wall with her back. Her lungs screaming for air, she crumbled to the floor. Unable to comprehend the event, her mind became suspended. Her entire body sobbed and she closed her eyes in an attempt to remain in control.

"Beccs!"

Rebecca heard her name and opened her eyes. She felt someone wrap around her, holding her tightly. The feeling was familiar and somehow she knew it was Donna. She could hear her saying something, but it was distant against the continuing sobs racking her body.

No . . . this wasn't happening . . . God, please no . . .

CHAPTER FOUR

They were almost home and he knew they had a long night ahead. Eric was concerned about the entire scenario. All bets were off and anything could happen. He knew Rebecca was a fighter and doing her best to stay strong, but even he realized a person can only take so much before they broke.

Eric's phone buzzed in his pocket and he lifted it, seeing Lug's name. "Hey, what's up?"

"How far out are you guys?"

"About a half an hour, why?"

"Hit the lights and get here in fifteen."

"Why, what's happened?"

"We received a 30 at Rebecca's office."

"What . . . who . . ."

"We don't know yet, first response just got onsite."

"Who called it in?"

"Donna."

They arrived twelve minutes later and it was everything he could do to remain calm. They flashed their badges and stepped into the elevator. He was trapped in his head, all of the swirling images of her bombarding him at once. He couldn't breathe. He shifted and looked to Adam whose face revealed his concern.

"You okay?" The elevator stopped and the doors opened.

Eric wordlessly moved into the familiar lobby. The office was filled with cops and security. He walked in search of her, scanning the room. He saw Rebecca's bodyguards shaking their heads looking pale. Next was Misty and the crime scene unit in Rebecca's office. The coroner wheeled a plastic covered body down the hall. Eric stopped, his entire body turning cold and heavy.

"Stiles!"

Lug exited a room in the corner.

Eric's body wouldn't budge. Lug jogged toward him, somehow knowing the terror-filled images pounding at him.

"She's okay."

Oxygen fill Eric's lungs and his heart restarted.

"The paramedics are checking her out now, but she's fine."

"Who was it?" Adam asked.

"Mindy Kramer."

Eric took a step back in anguish. "What happened?"

"Right now all we have are pieces. When we got here, our two guys were on the floor, unconscious. Donna and Rebecca were in the office along with Mindy's body. She was seated in the desk chair, her throat was cut and there was a note attached to her shirt."

"Has Rebecca been able to tell you anything?"

"Not yet," Lug said. "She hasn't said anything since we got here."

"What about Donna, was she able to tell you anything about what happened?"

"The only thing she could tell us was when she arrived, she found Rebecca in the office. To her it looked as if Rebecca had just found Mindy's body."

"Oh God . . ." Eric stepped away and saw her two bodyguards talking to a third officer. "How the hell did he get in here, Lug?"

"Where were her guards?" Adam added.

"I don't know," Lug replied with equal frustration. "At

this point, you guys know as much as I do."

"Let's get to work."

An hour later Eric was talking with the first responders.

"Detective Stiles," an unnamed officer called.

"Yeah?"

"There is someone downstairs asking to see you. He says he's your brother."

"Okay, thanks." A heaviness settled in his chest. He glanced at Adam before he took the elevator down to the ground floor.

"Eric!"

He walked to the barrier of security and met Charlie on the other side.

"What's going on, where's Rebecca?"

"She's okay. She's upstairs."

"You're sure?"

"Yes, I'm sure," Eric reassured a flash of heat coursing through him. "She's with Donna and the paramedics."

"You said she was okay?"

"She is, it's routine, I promise."

"What's going on? What is all of this?"

"I . . . uh . . . I can't tell you, Charlie. Not yet."

"What?"

"I understand you're concerned, but—"

"Something happened, he came after her again, didn't he?"

"Charlie . . ."

"I thought you were taking care of this! I thought she was safe?"

"She is—"

"No she's not, Eric! You put two armed officers on her and he still got to her! You're telling me you think this is safe?"

"No I don't, but it's the best we can do right now," Eric replied, wrangling his own temper against his brother's spouting. "We're going to catch this guy."

"When? When she's dead and this guy doesn't have anyone to torture?" Charlie spat back at him with venom. "I want to see her."

"You can't. Not right now, Charlie," Eric stepped in front of him.

"The hell I can't! Get out of my way, Eric," Charlie raged, trying to push past his brother.

"Charlie, stop!"

Charlie's temper boiled over and he swung at Eric.

Eric felt Charlie's fist connect with his jaw. A burst of light exploded in front of his eyes and then died. Eric recovered, but was too late to stop the three officers tackling his brother to the ground.

"Back off, stop," Eric commanded. They hauled Charlie off the floor and he met his brother's eyes. "Are you done?"

"Not even close," Charlie growled.

He stepped toward Eric, his eyes an emotional mess. Eric stood his ground, his own subdued temper flaring. He took a breath and walked away from him.

"Eric!"

"No! Not until you cool off!" Eric moved back to the elevator and went upstairs. The doors opened and Eric stepped off, meeting Adam.

"What's going on?"

"Charlie's downstairs."

"Is he alright?"

"Yeah he's fine. He just needs to cool off."

"Lug is asking for us."

"What's going on?"

"They want to move Rebecca to a safe house."

"Let's go." The two navigated through the room to the

small area in the corner Lug had taken over. It was a direct path to the room where Rebecca was being held. They weren't taking any chances.

"So what's the plan?"

"We've set up a room downtown," Lug explained. "We'll have hotel security and men on the floor and in the room. We have a team onsite making the arrangements. Everything should be ready within the hour."

"What's our exit strategy?"

"I'll lead with Andrews. Matheson and Stiles will escort Ms. Gailen and Ms. Smith in their vehicle. We'll have one black and white escort to bring up the rear. It'll take forty-five minutes to reach the hotel. We'll take them in through the kitchen and up the staff elevator. Room is on fifteen, our guys will be waiting for you at the elevator," Lug explained and his phone rang. "Be ready to go in ten."

"Stiles, I'll go get the car."

Eric nodded and then looked to Lug before he moved to the elevator.

"What are you doing?"

"Going to get Charlie." The rest of the ride was spent in silence. Eric stepped off the elevator and went to look for his brother. He found him pacing in the corner. "Charlie!" Eric waved him over and he joined him.

"Hey, look, Eric . . ."

"Don't worry about it," Eric brushed off in an even tone. "We are getting ready to move Rebecca and Donna to a more secure location. I figured you'd want to see her before they left."

"Where are you taking her?"

"I can't tell you." They stepped onto the elevator. "It will only be for a few days until things calm down."

"Eric, what's going on?" Charlie asked in fearful concern.

Eric's chest tightened. "Mindy's dead, Charlie," Eric said,

unable to ease the bluntness of the statement. "Rebecca was here when it happened. She found the body." His brother stood silent and pale, staring in disbelief.

"How . . . how is she?"

"I don't know. I haven't seen her." The elevator doors opened and he stepped out. "You aren't going to . . ." Eric glanced back and saw Charlie standing frozen in the elevator. "Charlie, what are you doing?" Eric asked and when he received no response, his chest flared. "Charlie!" The door began to close and he held it open, staring at his brother. "Charlie, wake up! She needs you."

"Eric, I don't . . ."

"Yes you do," Eric insisted, pulling him out of the elevator. "She's exhausted and terrified. She just found one of her best friends dead in her office."

"Exactly . . . I don't . . ."

"Look, she doesn't need you to fix this or even make it go away," Eric replied in a reassuring tone. "She just needs you to hold her . . . let her know you're here and it is going to be okay. Do you think you can do that?"

Charlie seemed to shake of the dazed look and nodded in agreement.

"I just need to be there."

"Right."

"I can do this."

"Okay, let's go." He led Charlie back to where Rebecca and Donna were waiting. He looked to Lugow and received a nod of approval. Eric grabbed the handle and pushed the door open. He scanned the immediate area and found her huddled on a couch in the far corner of the room. Her eyes lifted and saw him. She rose from the couch, her face a mask of pain, her eyes screaming at him in anguished desperation.

Beccs . . .

Charlie stepped into the room behind him. Her eyes dimmed and shifted before her arms wrapped around her body.

"Beccs, thank God!" Charlie rushed into the room and pulled her into his arms.

Her eyes remained steady until Charlie pulled her against him. Her eyes closed and a torrent of tears slid down her cheeks. It was everything Eric could do to not respond to her silent anguished plea. His gaze shifted and met with Donna's. She stared him down, scolding him with her eyes.

Everything was a blur of sound and motion until the door opened and she saw him. For a moment, her entire body sighed in relief. Then everything fell apart again. It was like the upward swing of an axe, where there was still a breath of hope until its weight fell in crushing force.

Charlie's arms around her made the pain so much worse. She tried to hide the agony, but it stung her cheeks with burning wetness. When she opened her eyes, again Eric was gone.

Charlie was gentle, reassuring and regretful. She tried to absorb the comfort he offered, but she was raw and didn't think anything could ever bring her comfort again.

Rebecca wasn't sure how much time passed when Lugow appeared. He explained due to the current situation, he felt it was best to move them to a secure location for a few days. Rebecca made no comment, she just listened and nodded.

Now it was time to go.

Charlie said he would see her in a few days. Eric reappeared along with several uniformed officers. Donna latched herself to her arm and Eric led the entourage out of the building. Once they hit fresh air, the women were led into the back of a sedan. Rebecca slid in and Donna followed. The door closed and a moment later, Eric got in the passenger's seat. Rebecca heard him say something over the radio and after a moment, they were moving.

She tried to focus on the scenery, playing a game of guessing where exactly they were headed. The image of Mindy's dead eyes and sliced neck was permanently burned into her mind. It became the background for every passing thought, breath and sigh. It would never go away, she would live with the guilt forever.

Mindy is dead because of me

Mike . . .

"We need to call Mike," she said, looking to Donna.

"I'll take care of it as soon as we get to the hotel."

"I want to talk to her parents," she continued, her mind having fixed on something tangible. "We have to go get George. He'll run out of food and I . . ."

"Beccs, it's okay we'll take care of everything, I promise." She put a soothing arm around her shoulder.

Rebecca went back to staring out the window and then they arrived. They pulled in the back, but there was no mistaking the landscape, they were at the Bellagio. The car stopped and they waited until two other vehicles joined them before Eric and Adam got out of the car.

Adam opened the back door on his side, facing the door of the building. Donna slid out first, followed by Rebecca. The uniformed officers reappeared and they entered the hotel and were led through the kitchen. They stopped at the elevators and waited. The doors opened and Eric and Adam stepped on with them, but only two officers in addition to them.

Another ten minutes and they had stepped off the elevator and were walking into the room. They took a quick look around before Donna led her into the bedroom. She sat on the bed and Donna disappeared into the bathroom. She wanted to curl up and fall asleep, but her body wouldn't move. She wondered if she would ever sleep again. Hopelessness began to creep over her and she started to tremble. Her lungs clenched and she gasped.

"Beccs," Donna said re-entering the bedroom. "Breathe, sweetie. Beccs,` you have to breathe."

Struggling for air, Rebecca locked onto her friend's voice. She forced herself to calm and her lungs relaxed, allowing the air to pass freely again. Donna took her hand, coaxing her off the bed.

"I drew you a bath," she said, leading her into the bathroom. "Do you want me to help you get undressed?"

Rebecca nodded, seeing the spacious tub and marble tiled floor. She heard the door close and glanced back at Donna. Rebecca took in the room. She made a mental note of where everything was, all of the doors, cabinets and any darkened corners where someone could hide. Her body started to involuntarily tremble again and Donna pushed her hair off her shoulder.

"It's okay, sweetheart. Just try and relax." Donna grabbed the robe off the door.

Rebecca took a breath and began to peel the clothing from her shaking body. Donna handed her the robe and Rebecca pulled it around her. She twisted her hair into a bun at the top of her head before moving to face her. "Okay, you're all set. Do you want me to help you get in?"

Rebecca shook her head, eyeing the tub. Donna ran a hand over her back with the smile before she moved to the door.

"I'll be right outside if you need anything, okay?"

She nodded and Donna disappeared behind the door. She scanned the room, a shiver running through her. She slipped into the sweet smelling heated water. It enveloped her like a blanket and she could feel her muscles begin to relax. She leaned her head back against the side of the tub, but refused to close her eyes. Her mind continued to be sluggish and unfocused. She tried to rein herself in, but her thoughts continued to be of nothing and everything. Her eyes closed despite herself.

She wanted it to stop

She had to make it stop

Her mind continued to spin out of control

"How can you have any clue as to what I need?" Rebecca *snapped in weary frustration. "It's easy to say, Beccs relax, or Beccs you need to sleep, or even Beccs calm down when you're not the one being tortured!"*

"I understand . . ."

"You have no idea, Mindy! You got off lucky with a box of blood! Try seeing your entire life covered in the stuff! You're not living through this, I am! So stop acting sympathetic because I don't want it or need it!" Rebecca thrashed at her in fueled rage. It wasn't meant for Mindy, but it was directed at her as she was the only one around. "I have work to do. So either focus on the task at hand or go home and play the damsel in distress! I'll call Charlie and tell him to get his white horse ready."

"That is a welcome change from being the self-centered heartless bitch you've turned into!" Mindy's voice growled at her.

Rebecca looked up in confusion.

"All I wanted was a chance with him. All I wanted was a chance at true love, but you couldn't give it to me, could you! You just can't let anyone be happy if it doesn't suit you! Right, Beccs?"

"Mindy, no I am so sorry I didn't . . ."

"Shut up, you lying treacherous bitch!"

Rebecca's eyes opened. The water surrounding her had cooled. She lifted herself out of the tub, wrapping the thick robe around her body. She walked to the mirror, staring at her muted reflection. She looked like death warmed over. Rubbing her hands over her tired eyes, she took a deep breath. Her eyes lifted and she saw Mindy standing just behind her, blood pouring out of her neck, her eyes cold and angry.

"I'm sorry, Mindy. I'm so sorry . . ." she said, pleading for the illusion's forgiveness, her body rocking in agony. Crumbling to her knees in uncontrolled sobs, she couldn't feel anything but pain and regret.

"Beccs . . ." Rebecca lay on the floor, curling herself into a ball of unrelenting agony. Donna took a seat next to her, and when Rebecca opened her eyes, she was face to face with her on the floor. "It's going to be okay."

"No it's not. Not now, not ever."

Eric closed the door and Donna led her to the back bedroom and they disappeared. An hour later, Lugow knocked on the door.

"How are we doing in here?"

"So far so good," Adam replied and Eric remained silent, leaning against the far wall.

"Okay, let's talk about what happens next," Lug said and they gathered in the living room.

Eric and Adam relayed what happened at the hospital and Lug pulled something from his jacket pocket.

"We have a new problem."

"What?" Adam took the paper and unfolded it.

Eric saw a sketch of a balding narrow faced man. "That's not Marco."

"Exactly."

"This is the description Ken gave you?"

"This is the guy he says took the photos and brought the buckets of blood to the apartment."

"So Marco has an accomplice. He could still be involved."

"Could be, but we have nothing to support it," Lugow replied in a logical calm tone. "We need to go with what we know and this guy is our best lead."

"Did Ken give you anything else?"

"Yeah, he said this guy likes breakfast," Lugow replied. "He is always bringing home the placemats from the Waffle House."

"Which one? There are at least a dozen locations just downtown." Adam asked.

"We should start at the one closest to the apartment and work our way out," Eric suggested when he heard the bedroom door open and Donna appeared. She met his eyes and he took the hint. She wanted him to follow. Adam and Lugow began mapping out the strategy. Eric excused himself from the conversation and followed Donna to the second bedroom. He walked in and she closed the door. "How's Beccs?"

"She's awful, Eric! How do you think she is?" she snapped in a hushed tone, turning away from him.

"Don, I . . ."

"What the hell are you doing?"

"Excuse me?"

"Are fucking blind? No you're not, I know you're not. I saw the look on your face when you opened that door! And you saw the way she looked at you!"

"I don't—"

"Yes you do, because you were in as much agony as she was when it was Charlie holding her and not you!" she stabbed at him without restraint. "Why are you doing this? Hasn't she been through enough?"

"I'm not doing anything!"

"You're right and that is the whole problem," she barked, challenging his confusion. "Eric, you being here and doing nothing is worse than if you weren't here at all!"

"What do you want me to do, Donna, leave?"

"Yes!"

"What?" he exclaimed in shock.

"God help us both if she ever finds out, but damn it, Eric,

she's in love with you! One-hundred percent, no holds bar, no going back, in love with you! So every time she sees you and you do nothing, it breaks her heart all over again," she explained.

He looked away, unable to gulp away the tightening in his chest.

"I know you didn't mean for any of this to happen, but it did and now we have to deal with it. So I am asking you, if you love her, you need to decide once and for all."

"Decide what?"

"You need to either step in or step out, Eric. You can't have both," she replied.

He pushed his hands through his hair.

"Either you are going to be with her, or you're not. If you choose you're not because of some sense of duty or honor, fine, great, whatever, but then you need to stay away. You need to disappear because you are hurting her more than you are helping."

The statement hit him hard and he struggled to remain in control. He knew she was right and it killed him. He didn't know what he was doing anymore. He'd forgotten all of the reason's he'd pushed her away, but still couldn't bring himself to betray his brother.

"But for heaven's sake, if you love her like I think you do," she said in a pleading tone, "stop fighting it. She needs you, Stiles. She's scared to death and carrying around all of this guilt, convinced all of this is her fault. Now, I can talk to her until I am blue in the face, but I know for a fact the only one she will listen to and even attempt to believe is you."

"I wish it were that easy, but—"

"How much are you going to put her through before you figure it out? You and Rebecca started something far away from here. It had nothing to do with Charlie. I know he's your brother, but we all know it's over between them. She never cared for him in that way and he knows it, even if he doesn't want to admit it. So the way I see it, the only person standing in your way, is you."

He and Adam returned to the station without a word to anyone. Adam allowed him to stew, no questions asked. Being his partner and friend, he somehow knew he was there to work. Mindless, monotonous work to help him push through the numbness enveloping him.

After a few hours, Eric's mind had begun to clear and he felt restless. He rose from his desk and walked back into the locker room. A nagging pulled at the back of his mind. He opened his locker and dug in the back for a pack of cigarettes he'd hidden for emergencies. He felt around and pulled them out with a handful of receipts.

He walked toward the garbage, glancing at the bits of paper. Scanning each of them before he tossed them away, a word caught his eye mid-toss and he stopped. Focusing on the flimsy faded piece of paper, he realized it was his receipt from the coffee shop. The memory crushed him and he tossed it into the garbage. He turned back to the locker, the pack of stale cigarettes in his hand. He stared at the painted metal for a moment.

He hadn't wanted any of it, he was content being a chauvinistic pig and not attached to anything, and then she dropped into his life. He hadn't been able to get her out of his head since the moment they'd met, and now he'd gotten what he thought he'd wanted all along. Donna handed him an out.

You need to disappear because you are hurting her more than you're helping . . . You and Rebecca started something far away from here. It had nothing to do with Charlie . . . the only person standing in your way, is you

Eric tried to breathe, but the numbness cocooning him shattered and left only intense rage and pain. He swung his fist forward, slamming the door of the locker shut. Pushing against it, he lost himself in the release of denial he'd let consume him. He unloaded all of his guilt and frustration onto the metal, the noise pounded in his ears, but he continued until there was nothing left.

"Stiles!"

Someone pulled him away from the metal.

"Stop, Stiles!"

Strong arms ceased his movement. He fought to break free. His chest heaved. They released him and he spun. Adam stared back at him. He avoided his friend's gaze, grabbed the crumpled pack of cigarettes and walked out of the locker room.

Chapter Five

He was on her and she couldn't move. She fought to get away, but her body wouldn't move. She managed to look to her left and saw Eric's peaceful sleeping face. She opened her mouth to call for him, but nothing came out.

He was ripping at her clothes, her skin, and she could feel the sting of his hands tearing at her body. A blinding pain thrust into her and she screamed . . .

Terrified to move, all of the muscles in her body went rigid. Her eyelids shot open in the dark of the room. Her heart pounding, panic filled her stomach. She tried to breathe, but the air wouldn't come.

She berated her mind for being so weak, telling her body to move. After a rush of air filled her lungs, it did. First her hand, her arm and then her legs. Each piece of her awakened and the images replaying in her mind fell away. She broke free of them and turned onto her back.

In a rush of unexpected emotion, the tears came hard and fast. Unable to stop them, she curled into herself, begging her mind for control.

Stop it . . . Stop it . . .

She pushed her hands through her hair and rolled out of the bed. She took a seat on the floor across from the bathroom. Her knees pulled to her chest, she struggled with the images of blood and death.

She hated feeling like this. She was beginning to wonder if she'd ever feel like a normal person again. She sat silent, her mind continuing to spin out of control.

She'd been such a blubbering idiot. So damn emotional and she was tired of it. She wanted her backbone to return, but every time she began to feel a little stronger, something happened to shut her down again.

While she'd never admit it aloud, she was exhausted and terrified. The only place she'd ever found any comfort was within his embrace and it was something she could never have again.

She rose from the floor and saw the leather jacket lying on the back of the chair. She pulled it on, hugging herself into it like a security blanket. She walked to the window and propped herself on the air conditioner. Her forehead rested on the cool pane of glass and she pulled her legs to her chest.

She thought back to the morning in Dallas, when she'd woken up in his arms. It seemed like forever ago, but she could still remember how difficult it was to leave.

She remembered the first glimpses of sunlight peeking through the curtains, surrounding them in an unbelievable cocoon of tranquility. Even after everything she'd been through with Lucy, in his embrace, she felt her soul sigh in contentment. She recalled his serene chiseled face shadowed in deep slumber. She'd never see him again and her heart protested. The thought hurt and she decided it would be easier to disappear than to have to say goodbye to him. She wanted to preserve the perfect memory, without pain or regret.

If it was anyone else . . .

A soft knock at the door startled her out of her thoughts. The door opened and she shifted in apprehension. His form was silhouetted against the light, but her heart knew who it was.

"Aren't you supposed to be asleep?"

"Probably." She turned back to the window. "What are you doing here? Come to check on your helpless victim?"

"You're anything but helpless, Beccs."

"Nice try, I might have bought that one a week ago."

"Beccs—"

"Needless to say, with the exception of a case of insomnia, I am fine," she lied, desperate to keep the rising emotion out of her voice. He moved into the room toward her. "No need to worry, I'm done falling apart."

"You're not fine."

"Earlier Charlie was trying to talk about anything but . . ." She slid off the air conditioner. Focusing on her balance, she hesitated, her voice trembling. She wiped at the moisture surrounding her eyes in irritation. "He said he wants to start a pool tournament at the Rustic. I'm not sure I want to go there though, I think I like being anonymous."

"Rebecca . . ."

She saw him move closer, his warmth calling to her. "I make more money that way." She realized he was standing beside her. She lifted her gaze to his in disbelief. He took a step closer. His fingertips lined her face. She closed her eyes with his touch and felt the unexpected warmth of his lips against hers. A gentle caress, a coaxing of her lips became an intense demand, weakening her knees.

His lips disappeared and her head reeled. Her eyes opened and met his gaze. He searched her face, reaching into her thoughts. She wanted to hide in his embrace, pull him around her and never let go, but she knew better. "What are you doing?" she asked him, suppressing the sob in her chest.

"Taking you back," he replied in a throaty whisper, his determination insulting and stirring her in the same instant.

"Who says I was ever yours to begin with?" She tried to push out of his embrace.

"Don't do this, Rebecca," his voice full of desperate frustration.

"I'm not doing anything," she defended sharply. His lips just a breath away, she struggled to steady her voice against her racing heart.

"Beccs . . ."

"This is what you wanted," she said, her voice cracking in emotion. "Nothing has changed."

"You're right, nothing's changed."

She tried to look away but he refused to let her.

"I just woke up and realized it."

"We made a decision—"

"No, I made a mistake. I should've never pushed you away."

"But you did!" she pushed back, her voice rising in anger. "You told me to forget Dallas, to forget what we . . . were, to protect Charlie! That's what you wanted, Eric."

"I know I—"

"You can't just change your mind!" She broke free of his loving embrace, unleashing her fear and anguish onto him. "What am I supposed to do? Believe you and hope you don't change your mind again when you decide—"

"Rebecca, stop . . ."

"He's your brother. I won't be the one to come between you. I've destroyed enough!" She began to crumble, the words tumbled without thought.

"No . . . no . . . you haven't done anything wrong, sweetheart," he said, his eyes pleading with her to listen. "This isn't your fault, none of this is your fault."

"I can't . . . Eric . . . he's your brother!"

"You're right, he's my brother, but I won't let him take you away from me. You belong with me, not him."

Startled by his words, she turned to face him. "I'm not worth you—"

"The hell you're not!" he objected, his hands pushing into her hair, pressing his forehead to hers. "Beccs, every moment I haven't been able to kiss you, hold you, or touch you, has been a moment in hell. I need you and not just part of you, I need all of you."

She stood within his hands, his warmth coursing through her without restraint. All she could hear was the pounding of her own heart and she hesitated in releasing her defenses, unable to believe it was happening. She felt him shift, his lips brushing against her forehead.

"Please tell me I haven't lost you." His voice was thick and unsteady, his arms encircling her waist. "I can't do this without you."

She closed her eyes and took a breath. Tears slid down her cheeks. Every piece of hope long since buried re-emerged. She let go of all the reasons they couldn't and clung to all the reasons they should.

Rebecca lifted her eyes, saw the torture etched in his face. She raised herself onto her toes and pressed her lips to his. She kissed him with all the love and tenderness she could convey. He crushed her against him, possessing her mouth with slow thoughtful kisses. The remnants of her defenses fell away, leaving her heart exposed and wanting. It was heaven and she reveled in it, until reality hit her hard in the chest. She pulled back and looked up at him, her heart pounding in protest.

"What?" he asked, stroking her cheek with his thumb in concern.

"We can't do this to Charlie, not now. Not with everything that's happened. Eric . . ."

"Listen to me." He pulled her closer, forcing her to look at him. "I need you to not worry about this right now."

"How am I—"

"I need you to trust me to handle it."

She diverted her eyes, the strain in her chest growing with the guilt.

"He's my brother, this is between us. I will take care of it."

"So I am supposed to just sit here while you take a

sledgehammer to your relationship with him?"

"I know it's going to be hard, but I have to believe Charlie will understand." He smoothed the curls around her face. "We can't do this anymore, sweetheart, it's too much. Especially now . . ."

"I'm fine, we can wait . . ." she protested, despite her inability to restrain the tears of raw pain slipping down her cheeks.

"Rebecca, he needs to know the truth."

She searched his eyes for any sign of doubt and nodded in agreement. He pulled her into his chest. Her cheek rested against his heart and she felt him kiss the top of her head. She let her defenses fall and clung to him. His warmth wrapped around her like a protective blanket. It was the safest she'd ever felt and her heart opened.

"Beccs."

She realized she was trembling. She looked up at him, unable to hold back the rushing of fear and anguish overwhelming her. "Eric . . ." The sobs pushed from her chest, unrestrained, and her entire body shook.

"Baby, it's going to be okay. I promise it's going to be okay."

His arms around her, he shifted before lifting her into his embrace. She hid in the small area between his neck and shoulder, her mind collapsing uncontrolled. All of the fear, anguish and guilt she'd buried erupted from every pore of her being.

She clung to him and keeping his arms around her, he laid her down with him on the bed. He held her close and she continued to release all of the buried sobs she'd been collecting since the nightmare began.

After a long while, her body buckled in exhaustion and she melted into his warmth. She was safe and warm, his steady heartbeat against her cheek and she felt herself fall into a deep comforting slumber.

Her sobs slowed into whimpers and she fell asleep in his arms. He watched her sleep, his mind playing out all of the possible scenarios ahead of them. He needed to talk to Charlie. He needed to keep her safe. The situation had risen too far out of control and he needed to put a stop to it.

He felt her shift against him, and his mind began to wake from its peaceful calm. His arms instinctively pulled her closer. Her warm soft body filled him with a sated breath.

He felt her stir again and a soft touch along his chin pulled a smile from his lips. He opened his eyes and found her beautiful gaze staring back at him. She reached out, her fingertips tracing the line of his cheek before lining his lips.

"I thought it was a beautiful dream," she admitted in a soft whisper.

The statement took his breath away and he realized how horrible a mistake he had made. He broke her heart when all he'd wanted from the moment he touched her was to love her.

"Dream or not, I'm never leaving you again," he said in a hushed breath before he dipped his head down to caress her lips. They were soft and sweet, a candy he could never resist. She pulled him in, her nails curling up his neck into his hair. Their kisses turned fervent, emotion mixing with lust.

His fingers wrapped in her hair and she pulled him against her. He consumed her mouth, his tongue teasing her lips. His hand trailed down, grasping the bottom of her shirt. He lifted himself slightly before he pushed the hem of the shirt upward. She immediately raised her arms and he quickly pulled it over her head, her hair spilling onto the pillow.

He crushed her mouth again, taking her hands in his and pushing them down beneath his into the bed. She squeezed his hands back in wanting and he left her mouth, trailing kisses across her collarbone, to her sternum and down her abdomen. When he reached the top of her jeans, he looked up at her in awe. Her eyes were closed, her body writhing in want.

She was so unbelievably beautiful his heart was bursting with passion. He went to work on her jeans and within a few agonizing seconds, pulled them down her legs. Retracing his kisses from the top of her lace underwear all the way to the swell of her breasts, he stopped and lifted his head. Her hands wrapped in his hair, pulling him back up to her mouth and she devoured him whole. His right hand once again entangled itself in her soft hair, his left hand made steady work of caressing the soft skin beneath him.

She clawed at his back and he smiled when she whimpered. She broke the kiss and looked at him with lust-filled eyes, "No fair, Stiles, you're cheating."

Her hand ran down his chest, swiftly reaching his belt, she kept his eyes locked with hers. He teased her with breathed kisses. Her hands undid his belt and unbuttoned his pants. Her soft hand hit the skin of his lower abdomen and hesitated a moment. She wrapped her warm hand around his engorged cock and squeezed, her thumb teasing the line along the head.

He lost his breath and where he expected her to smirk at him, her eyes smoldered and she pushed herself against him. Their mouths were attached again. She stroked him within the confines of his pants. Her touch pushing him to the edge, he had to concentrate to hold himself back.

She managed to wiggle out from beneath him and using the leverage of her leg, rolled him onto his back. Her hair fell in a cascade of silk around him. She tongued his mouth. She trapped his cock against the warmth between her legs, stroking him with her pelvis. She undid the buttons of his shirt. Her mouth trailed across his collarbone, down his chest and stopped just above his stomach. She tugged on a section of cloth at his hip.

The pants disappeared and so did she for a moment. Her hand encircled his cock and within seconds, the warmth of her mouth wrapped around his head, her tongue glazing the tip. Her hand pumping the base, her lips made their way down and then back up. She would stop every few strokes to tease the bundle of nerves behind the head and then slid him back down her throat. The luscious manipulation was steadily driving him toward ecstasy. A primal moan emanated from his chest and he knew he would be able to take very little of this. He rose up on his arms and gently pulled her up to meet his mouth, his hands tracing the curve of her body. Her naked legs straddled his groin and he thought he was going to explode.

Discarding his shirt, he slid his left hand around her waist and moved up to the clasp of her bra. With a flick of his thumb, it came undone and he pulled the strap over her left shoulder and down her arm. It fell away, revealing the cherry of a nipple hiding beneath. Eric savored the beauty of it. His hands braced her and she leaned back, laying herself out for his consumption. His hunger for her swelled. He started at the hollow of her neck, trailing heated kisses across her chest. He took a red bud in his mouth, suckling and teasing it with his tongue. She dug into his shoulders, her lace covered warmth once again sliding against him. He swirled his tongue over the nipple encased within his mouth. Teasing it to erection with every stroke, his thumb went to work on her right nipple. His mouth switched sides while his hand trailed down her stomach to where their bodies met and began to massage her clit.

She trembled beneath his multiple conquests, and as he roused her passion, his own grew stronger. Lifting herself back to him, she teased his lower lip. Her hips relentlessly manipulated his cock bringing his breath in short gasps of increasing desire.

His hand entangled itself back into her hair. Her kiss, heated and wanting, fueled his own fire and he once again captured a rosy nipple in his mouth. Her head fell back and she raised her hips.

"Eric, please . . ."

With her plea, his cock twitched and his balls tightened. He pushed her panties aside, shifted and swiftly impaled her pussy. She cried out in pleasure. He groaned, the heat of her cunt sending a flash of lightning through his body. She began to ride him, his hands curling around her sweet ass.

She met his eyes and he could see his world unfold within their heat. She kissed him, her body continuing to move. His hands moved down her back and around to her waist, firmly grasping her hips. Bruising her soft flesh with his fingers, her velvet kisses and teasing hips pulled him along and he could feel the pressure building inside his groin.

Her body continued to pull increased flashes of ecstasy from him and he thrust himself upward, crashing into her. Her head fell back with a gasp and the fire within him raged. Overcome by the exquisiteness of her body, his unrelenting love for her burst forth, unfettered. He thrust into her again and she cried out. She devoured his mouth with matched passion while she continued to grind against him.

Releasing his restraint and desperately wanting to push her over the edge with him, his thumb circled her clit, his mouth greedily suckling on her delectable nipple. He could sense the pressure in her body steadily rising. Her breaths became shorter. Her pussy pulsed around him, massaging his wanting cock. Bolts of molten fire coursed through his groin, every stroke pushing him closer to the edge.

"Eric . . ." she said, pleading for him with a wanting breath.

In a flash of heat, he plowed himself into her again. His hands lifted her ass, his groin began a controlled piston of thrusts. She trembled under his hands.

His cock swelled in delight and his body exploded within her. His world lifted into a siren of light and heat before it crashed back into his body.

He held her tight against him, their labored breaths joined in the need for oxygen. She framed his face with her hands, staring down into his eyes. She laid her soft lips on his and he kissed her with a sweet tenderness. He lifted his legs, laying her down on the bed beneath him. He teased her lips while his fingers played with her hair.

"God, I missed you so much." He kissed her again. Her heavy eyes smiled back at him and he shifted onto his side. She turned, pressing her soft back against him and he pulled the blankets around them. His arm wrapped snugly around her and she laced her fingers within his, pulling him closer. He nuzzled her ear and kissed her neck before kissing the top of her head.

"Don't leave me, Eric," she said in a small fragile voice.

"Never again, Beccs. Never again."

Chapter Six

They'd made the decision together. Eric was going to talk to Charlie at the next available opportunity. The problems began when the violent crimes unit was hit with another set of murders. Eric spent the next four days in the field or at the station. He checked in with her often, but wasn't able to break away until the morning of Mindy's funeral.

While they didn't expect anything to happen, it was going to be Rebecca's first public outing since the murder. Donna and Lugow tried to talk her out of going, but she stubbornly refused. When Eric attempted to broach the subject, she shut him down. Thus they worked out a plan for the chapel and the burial. Given the turnout was expected to be large, Lugow and Donna had little trouble convincing Mindy's parents to have the reception at the Rustic.

The day was clear and bright, the desert winds soft and cooling for once. Eric stood just inside the door of the Rustic, anxiously awaiting their arrival. He hadn't been able to step away from the station until then. His chest hurt.

I should've been with her and yet instead once again . . .

From what Lugow said, the day had progressed without incident. Lug and Donna escorted Rebecca throughout the day. Lugow told him she seemed to be coping well. Eric also knew how good she was at hiding behind those electric eyes of hers.

So damn stubborn

Eric saw the truck pull into the parking lot and inhaled much needed oxygen. He still wasn't sure exactly how he was going to do this. He hadn't been able to talk to Charlie yet, which meant he needed to keep his distance. He wasn't convinced he'd be able to. Not today.

Not if she needed him.

Two black SUV's turned into the parking lot. After a few minutes, Lugow, Donna, Charlie and finally Rebecca exited the first vehicle. Harry, Mike, Fric and Frack exited the second. The group moved toward him. His eyes focused on her walking beside Charlie. She was wearing a navy blue skirt, suit and heels. Her beautiful hair was pulled away from her face and harnessed with a tie at the base of her neck. He searched for some indication of how she was doing, but the dark glasses covering her eyes prevented even a guess. He pushed open the door and Donna led them in. Eric restrained his instinct to reach for her and remained at arm's length.

The reception, while an event of mourning, was filled with laughter, tears and support. Charlie was kept busy with running the event while Rebecca stuck close to Donna and Harry. Eric, Lugow and Adam wandered and mingled, keeping an eye on everything and everyone.

The room held a constant hum of activity until a gasp echoed throughout and Eric turned.

"You bitch! It should've been you," he heard a woman say in a cracked anguished voice before she slapped Rebecca across the face.

"He should've cut your throat, not hers!"

Eric watched both Donna and Harry move, but Rebecca's hand raised to stop them.

"I'm so sorry, I . . ." Rebecca offered in a soft repentant voice, meeting the woman's eyes.

"You're sorry? You did this to her!" The woman lunged at Rebecca and Harry stepped in, holding the distraught woman back as Donna pulled Rebecca away. "You fucking killed my sister you *whore!*"

Mindy's family stepped in and moved to soothe the emotional woman. They pulled her away and Donna led Rebecca toward the back of the bar. Donna released her and Rebecca turned away. Another outburst of distraught emotion erupted within Mindy's family, causing distraction throughout. Rebecca's hand was in her hair, her face crinkling in agony. Eric made his way across the room, but before he could reach her, she grabbed her purse and ran for the door. Donna watched her go. She caught his eye and he headed for the same door. He stepped out and looked for her amongst the low shadows. He saw her leaning against his truck and jogged to meet her.

"Beccs."

She spun in fear and he caught her within his hands. She stopped, realized it was him and crumbled. Her entire body heaved, streams of tears falling down her cheeks.

"I did this . . ." she gasped in agony.

He instinctively pulled her into his chest. "No . . . Beccs . . ."

"I should've sent her away! Pushed her away from me and then she would be alive!" she ranted into his shirt.

"You didn't do this."

"I should have protected her, Eric!" she exploded, pushing away from him.

"Sweetheart, stop. This is not your fault!"

"I want to go back to the hotel."

"Okay, I'll—"

"No."

"What?"

"I want Lugow to take me," she started wiping away her tears in conviction. "I want you, Donna and Charlie to stay away. From me, from all of this . . ."

"Beccs—"

"No, Mindy's dead!" she protested, tears continuing to flow down her cheeks. "I am not . . . he's already gone after Donna. It is only a matter of time before he comes after you and Charlie!"

"Then we'll handle it—"

"No . . . I don't want to handle it," she barked in emotion fueled anger. "It's the only way—"

"No it's not—"

"Yes it is, it's the only way to keep you safe . . ." she plead in helpless desperation. "I just want it to stop . . . I'm so scared. I can't . . . Make it stop, please make it stop . . ."

"You need to just hang on a little longer, baby. I promise it is almost over." He pulled her within his embrace, kissing the top of her head.

"I can't . . . do this, Eric . . ." She shifted, looking up at him, her eyes tearing again. "It's too much . . . I don't want to be here . . . I can't . . ."

"Okay, how about this." He stepped back, tucking a rebel lock of her hair behind her ear. "Go back inside, say goodbye to Mindy's parents, my Dad and Charlie. I'll grab Lug and Donna and we will go back to the hotel."

She nodded in agreement, taking a deep breath.

He squeezed her hand, kissed her forehead and watched her walk back inside. He alerted the rest of the team they would be leaving within the next half hour via radio. He walked toward the door and Charlie stepped out. "Hey, Rebecca is ready to—"

Charlie's fist connected with his jaw.

Eric absorbed the blow and recovered. He faced his brother whose chest was heaving with rage. "Okay I deserved that, now let me explain." Eric straightened his back and Charlie lunged for him. Eric planted his feet, but his brother hit him full force in the ribs, throwing him back. The next thing he knew, Charlie was on top of him and he heard the door open and Rebecca's voice.

"Charlie, stop!"

Eric's eyes opened.

Rebecca pulled on Charlie's arm.

"Charlie no!" Eric warned, but Charlie jerked back will full force and Eric watched her fall back, hard onto the ground. The call got Charlie's attention. Eric threw a punch, connecting with his jaw.

Charlie fell back, stunned.

Eric got to his feet.

Rebecca was being helped off the ground by Donna and Lugow.

Eric's temper raged. He turned to Charlie, throwing a fist into his brother's stomach.

"Eric, *stop!*"

At Rebecca's voice, he forced himself to step back in restraint.

"You're taking advantage of her, Eric. I'm not going to let you do it!"

"That's not—"

"*Don't!*" Charlie growled, glaring at him. "So is this what you've been doing? You've been using her? Going behind my back instead of finding the psycho who is trying to hurt her?"

"Of course not!"

"You just couldn't let her be, could you? She's helpless and fragile and you just couldn't—"

"Charlie stop!" Rebecca objected.

"He does this, you know. He pretends to be the white knight, the protector. Until he gets you in bed and then . . ." Charlie goaded.

Eric took a few angry steps toward him.

"Eric, don't." Her hand wrapped around his. "He's upset."

"Boy he's really got you fooled, Beccs," Charlie quipped.

Rebecca turned to face him. "Charlie, just stop! This isn't Eric's fault, it's mine," she replied sternly. "So if you're going to be angry with anyone, be angry with me!"

"That's what he wants you to think, Beccs," Charlie pleaded. "You're smarter than this!"

"No one meant for it to happen this way. Please, just let us . . ." she started and then stopped. "If you would just let us explain . . ." She trailed off, her hand going into her hair.

"Explain what? How he took advantage you? How he lured you into bed with promises of protection and love. And you fell for it, didn't you?"

"You don't . . ."

"So how long has he been slipping into your bed? Hate to tell you, but danger and fear are a classic backdrop to the infamous Stiles seduction . . ."

"That's enough!" Eric roared, unbelieving of the words spilling from his brother's mouth.

"Charlie, please try . . ." Rebecca started.

Eric watched her take a deliberate step back. She turned to him, her face ashen. Her head fell back and he rushed to catch her thin form in his arms before she hit the ground. "Beccs!" He eased her down and her body abruptly curled in pain.

"Eric . . ." she gasped, clutching at his shirt in agony.

"Stay with me, Beccs," he said, watching her struggle. "Call an ambulance!"

She cried in pain, her body lurching in his arms.

"Rebecca." She met his eyes just before they closed and she went limp in his arms. "Beccs, stay with me, baby. Rebecca, can you hear me? Beccs!" His chest heavy in panic, he scooped her into his arms and rushed her inside.

"Eric, the pool table!"

He moved toward it and laid her down.

"The ambulance is five minutes out," Adam said.

"Come on, baby, wake up," he said, smoothing the hair away from her face, trying to get her to come back.

"Her heart is racing," Donna said.

He turned to Adam. "Where are they?" Eric glanced at his brother in utter fear. He looked around for his father and stopped. He saw the flash of a man's smiling face before the attached body turned to the back door. The face clicked in Eric's mind and he struggled with his next move.

"Lug . . ." Eric called, but he couldn't find him or Adam. Eric turned and looked to his brother and Charlie nodded. Eric tore through the bar and pushed through the back door. He saw the two officers posted in the back. "Where is he!"

One of the officers pointed.

Eric saw the man cross the parking lot. He took off after him and the two officers followed. "Get Lugow and Matheson, now!" Eric ordered. He saw the suspect take off in a run to a yellow Volkswagen bug. *"Stop police!"* Eric made it halfway.

The car started.

Eric positioned himself in front of it, his gun aimed at the windshield. *"Get out of the car!"* Eric commanded, seeing his two guys in his peripheral vision.

The car revved its engine.

"Get out of the car with your hands up!" Eric heard the tires squeal. The car bounded toward him and he fired twice. He jumped out of the way. He rolled onto his stomach and heard another six shots fired. Adam and Lugow blew out the tires. The car slowed to a stop and he surged to his feet and sprinted toward the driver's side of the car. Adam and Lugow were on either side, several feet behind.

The suspect leapt out of the car and took off in a run.

Eric kicked it into overdrive to make up the difference. Once he'd bridged the gap, he leapt forward and caught the suspect by the legs.

They crashed to the pavement together. The man tried to resist. Eric climbed up his torso. The man threw his arm out. Eric avoided it and sent a fist into his jaw. He fell back. Eric flipped him onto his stomach. He pushed a knee into his spine and pulled the man's arms taunt.

The suspect laughed aloud.

"You like pain, asshole," Eric pushed down a little harder on the man's back and pulled him by the arms. "What did you do to her?"

The man laughed harder.

Eric cuffed him and turned him over. He picked him up by the shirt. "*Tell me what you did!*"

"Sleeping beauty is such a nice fairy tale," the man mocked.

Eric lost his patience and dropped him to the ground before pounding his fist into the man's face.

"Stiles, stop . . ."

Eric heard buzzing in his ear.

"Stiles!"

He was pulled off the man. Adam and Lug took over. The sound of sirens made him turn. The ambulance pulled out of the parking lot. Eric looked back to Adam and Lug who seemed to understand. They nodded and Eric ran to his truck, following the ambulance to the hospital.

CHAPTER SEVEN

He was about half an hour behind them when he walked into the waiting room, searching for a familiar face. Donna saw him and moved to meet him. "How is she?"

"There's been no change, they're in with her now."

Eric tried to breathe.

"You need to leave," Charlie growled.

Eric turned to face him. "Charlie . . ."

"No, I mean it, Eric, you stay away from her!"

"Charlie, calm down," Donna said.

"You told me you would protect her! You told her—"

"I know I did!" Eric replied, his heart breaking with every beat.

"This is your fault, Eric! You did this!" Charlie growled again, stepping closer. "If you hadn't been so preoccupied with getting laid, this would have never happened!"

"Oh shut up, Charlie, you don't know what the hell you're talking about!"

"Unfortunately, I know all too well—"

"Okay, stop," Donna interjected. "Everyone is on edge so we all just need to take a step back and regroup."

Eric walked away, his mind spinning. The image of her clinging to him in pain stabbing at him.

Three hours later a doctor walked into the waiting room with an update.

"How is she?" Charlie asked the doctor.

Eric rose from the set of chairs and glanced toward Donna who moved to join him.

"Unfortunately, Ms. Gailen has been dosed or drugged. We don't know with what so we can only treat the symptoms," the doctor explained.

Eric's panic grew.

"We've introduced activated charcoal into her system. We've also given her an antagonist to help slow any further absorption. Her pulse has steadied and her O2 stats are fine."

"What happens now?"

"Well there isn't much more we can do except wait and see what happens."

"Can we see her?" Donna asked.

"Yes, but only one at a time, for now. Just until we can move her upstairs to a room," the doctor said.

Donna nodded. The doctor stepped away from the group. She looked to Eric and then to Charlie.

Eric glanced at Charlie and was met with a furious glare.

"Okay, look, you both need to hash this out before anyone goes in there," Donna said, looking to both men. "So take it outside or whatever, but figure it out, because neither of you are going to walk in there with this crap hanging overhead."

Eric followed Charlie out into the parking lot. He leaned against the wall, preparing himself for the lashing.

Charlie paced the small area beside the emergency room. "You bastard." Charlie faced Eric with accusing eyes. "How could you do this? How could you take advantage of her like this?"

"That's not how it happened."

"*I trusted you!*"

Eric did his best to just take the abuse, despite his own fraying nerves.

"She trusted you and now she's in there fighting for her life because of what? Because you just couldn't stay away from her? She was something you couldn't have and you just couldn't resist!"

"Charlie . . ."

"Fuck my brother, take advantage of the situation," Charlie continued.

Eric felt his temper getting the better of him.

"Take advantage of the woman who is depending on you. She's kind, caring, beautiful . . . oh, and vulnerable, so easy pickings, right? Despite knowing how I feel about her!"

"I tried to walk away, Charlie," Eric replied in defense. "We both did."

"Don't try to blame this on her—"

"I'm not. Charlie, you have to believe this is not the way we wanted this to happen."

"You wouldn't know her at all if it weren't for me!"

"That's not true."

"What are you talking about?"

"I met Rebecca on my way to the wedding," Eric explained without going into too much detail. "It was one night and I didn't think . . . we didn't think we would ever see each other again. We had no idea any of this—"

"You're lying!"

"I have no reason to lie to you." Eric shook his head in sincerity. "Please believe me when I say we never intended any of this to happen. I was planning to tell you myself, but—"

"Yeah the best of intentions is an easy statement after the fact, isn't it? You always have the best of intentions, don't you, Eric? Why can't you for once just tell me the truth!"

"Fine. The truth is, I tried. We tried to keep what happened from you! To ignore each other for your sake, but I can't do it anymore. " Eric replied in harsh frustration. "I'm sorry I hurt you. I am sorry you feel betrayed, but I can't . . . I can't step aside anymore. Especially now when she needs me the most. Charlie, she's everything to me! I can't . . . I won't walk away from her, not even for you." Eric watched the statement sink in before he turned and walked back into the hospital. His brother knew the truth. It was done. His only focus now was to see her.

Charlie walked in just behind him, his face still red in anger. After an hour of silence, they saw the emergency room door open and Donna stepped out.

"I'm going to see her," Charlie announced walking to the door, but she stopped him with her arm.

"Charlie, don't."

"Get out of the way."

"No," Donna replied. "I'm sorry, but she's asking for Eric."

"What?" Charlie's head dropped and he stepped back.

Donna met Eric's eyes and she nodded. She led him through the doors and they walked down the hall until they reached an elevator. She stopped and hit the button.

"Where are we going?"

"Third floor," Donna replied, her eyes focused on the elevator. "They moved her to a private room about ten minutes ago."

"Donna . . ." The elevator doors opened and they stepped in.

"She's not awake."

"What?"

"I lied."

"Why?"

"Because she needs you in there more than any of us," she replied, deep lines of concern ebbing her face. "I know I hurt Charlie, but I don't care. She loves you and she's going to need you there when she opens her eyes, not Charlie."

"Thanks, Donna." He pulled her into a hug and the doors of the elevator opened.

"Room 314. I'll make sure Charlie's okay."

"Thanks." Eric stepped off the elevator and started down the hall. He pushed the door open and all the air escaped his lungs. He was so relieved to just be able to see her, he ignored the monitors and cords surrounding her bed. He focused on the beauty of her sleeping face. He didn't know what to do or say so he did what came to him. He grasped her hand and leaned forward, placing a kiss on her forehead. The romantic in him expected to see her eyelids flutter open, but they didn't. The pang in his heart echoed in his mind.

The doctor arrived to check on her within the hour and told him she could wake up at any time. It could be hours or minutes. So Eric settled into the chair beside her bed and waited for his sleeping beauty to wake.

He wasn't sure how much time passed when he heard the door open and watched Donna move into the room with two cups of coffee. She handed him one while she pulled up a chair next to him. He nodded to her in thanks and noticed the extra cream. He took a sip, his gaze on Rebecca. "What time is it?"

"A little after three."

"Is it?"

"Yep."

"Is Charlie still here?"

"No," she replied, looking down at the floor. "Harry came by and we convinced him Rebecca needed rest and the best thing to do for now was to go home. I told them we would call as soon as we knew anything more."

Eric's gaze fell to the floor, remembering the betrayal shining in Charlie's eyes. He wondered how they were going to get past this.

"He's going to forgive you, Eric," Donna offered. "Yeah he is going to be a dick for a while and there may be some begging and bribery involved, but he'll see how much you love Rebecca and he'll accept it."

Eric couldn't help but grin at the comment and the mood in the room lightened a little.

How much you love Rebecca . . .

He'd avoided using the word, but realized how it encompassed his feelings for her. He was in love with her, there wasn't any denying it. He'd found the one his father spoke of and he was right.

You just know.

"Don't tell her I told you this, but Beccs is a shoe freak," Donna said, making Eric laugh aloud. "I'm sincerely warning you because she has, at last count, seventy-eight pairs of shoes. The list will grow. So you better have the bucks to support the habit because it could be a serious threat to your relationship."

"I'll keep that in mind."

"But seriously, and remember, this is her best friend talking," Donna started. "I've heard Beccs side of this *thing* you two have going on and now I want to hear yours."

"What do you want to know?"

"Whatever you want to tell me," she replied, sitting back in her chair.

"Well first off, I'm an idiot," he said, which made her stifle a laugh. "And I don't know . . . I'm captivated by her. She's the most beautiful, amazing, person I've ever known and I knew it the first time I saw her."

"In Dallas."

"Yeah, in Dallas," he replied, looking at her in curiosity. "Beccs told you."

"The night of Charlie's coming home party," she replied. "I understand why you decided to not tell anyone about Dallas, but what changed your mind? It couldn't just have been my scolding."

"Are you concerned I'm going to change it back?"

"No . . . actually I'm not. I am curious though."

"The night when Charlie introduced me to Rebecca, it was . . . surreal," he started to explain, thinking back over the rollercoaster of emotions he'd experienced in such a small amount of time. "Never in a millions years did I ever think I would see her again."

"Did you want to see her again?"

He stared down into his coffee, debating how forthcoming he was going to be. He glanced back at Donna and knew why she was Rebecca's best friend. She had a blunt but sideways way of looking at the world. "Yes. I hadn't been able to get her out of my head. So when she was standing there just feet away from me with Charlie's arm around her, I froze."

"So you both panicked and acted like nothing happened, thus the unspoken agreement was born."

"Pretty much," Eric admitted, feeling like an idiot for having put them all through hell. "Charlie was just so happy. I couldn't take it away from him. I'm his brother. I've always been the one to protect him. I knew if he ever found out, he would never forgive me. To be honest, my life isn't . . . easy. This isn't anything I would have ever expected or looked for."

"And now?"

"Now?" he repeated, rubbing the back of his neck. He stood up, thinking back over the past few weeks, his gaze landing on her beautiful face. "I can't . . . breathe without her."

"I can see how that might be a problem."

"I've never . . . I've never needed anything before. When she's not around, it feels like a piece of me is missing. It's crazy, to be honest, and we hardly know each other."

"Oh, I wouldn't say that," Donna replied with a gentle smile. "Sometimes you don't have to know everything about a person to have a connection with them. Take Rebecca and myself for example. We could finish each other's sentences and have a conversation without saying a word. A few months later, my dad died, and I would have never made through it without her. People come into our lives for a reason. Maybe you and Rebecca met in Dallas because someone knew she would need you or you would need her. Or it could be as simple as you are meant to be together."

"So I need to just go with it."

"If it feels right, why not?" Donna's phone beeped and she rose, excusing herself to answer it

Eric's gaze fell on Rebecca. He wished she would wake up so he could tell her everything. Tell her how much he needed her, how much he loved her. He kissed her hand and took a seat on the edge of the bed. His fingertips skimmed over her hair, a deep ache rising in his chest. He stroked her cheek with the back of his hand, silently begging her to open her eyes and come back to him.

She shifted.

His heart stopped and then restarted. "Beccs," he said, leaning closer, his fingertips resting against her temple.

She stirred again.

"Beccs, open your eyes."

She turned into the warmth of his hand. Her eyelids fluttered open, revealing the blue he craved.

"Hey, beautiful." She tried to focus on him and her face crinkled in unknown pain. "Hey, hey," he reassured, his heart ripping at the panic in her eyes. Tears began to run down her cheeks and he stroked her hair. "You're okay."

"Eric," she managed to say, her body shaking uncontrolled.

He lifted her into his arms, wrapping himself around her. "You're okay," he said into her hair, She clung to him and he tried to soothe her. "You're okay, sweetheart. It's over, he can't hurt you anymore."

Chapter Eight

The doctor and two nurses finished their poking and prodding and left her alone. Rebecca sunk down into the pillow, carefully considering what they'd told her about what happened. Someone dosed her. They still didn't know with what, but it shut her down and she ended up in the hospital.

Her head felt like a lead weight and ached. She struggled to go back to the last thing she remembered. She knew she was at the reception and she was upset about something, but everything else was a blur and too fuzzy to recall. The doctor said traces of the drug were still in her system. It could take up to three days before she was feeling like herself again. She wondered how it happened. She was at a funeral for Christ's sake, and how do you get poisoned and not know it?

She was confused and overwhelmed by fear when she'd first opened her eyes. Eric was there, waiting for her, and in the safety of his arms, she was able to just let go of everything. She could cry and he didn't care, he just held her close to him and told her it was going to be okay. In all her life, she'd never known the feeling of protection and complete security. Now it wrapped around her like a blanket and she wasn't sure what to do.

Her thoughts were heavy and she could sleep for another twelve hours, which she found ridiculous.

He can't hurt you anymore . . .

Was it over? Had they caught the man who did this?

The door opened she ordered her eyes to focus. Donna walked into the room with a wide smile.

"Hey, Beccs, nice of you to join us," Donna said, pulling her into a hug.

"I am so glad you're here."

"Where else would I be?" Donna replied. "How are you feeling?"

"I'm fine, just a little tired," she replied with a smile, annoyed at the frailty of her own voice.

"I bet you are." She took a seat on the bed across from her.

"Donna, tell me what happened."

"You don't remember?"

"The last thing I remember is being at the reception and upset about something," she replied, rubbing her forehead in frustration. "After that, it is all a little fuzzy."

"What's a little fuzzy?" Eric said. He walked into the room.

A crashing feeling of calm washed over her.

"Rebecca's memory."

"Well, what is the last thing you do remember?"

"Being upset at the reception," she replied with a nod.

Eric looked to Donna.

"What's going on? What are you two not telling me?"

"Beccs, we don't need to talk about this now," Eric said, sitting on the bed, taking her hand in his. "You've been through a lot and you need to rest, sweetheart."

"Don't you handle me, Eric Stiles!" she snapped at him and pulled her hand out of his in anger at his attempt placate her. "I may be sitting in a hospital bed, but you do not get to decide what I can and cannot handle!"

"Beccs . . ." Donna tried to interject.

"Tell me what's going on, Eric."

"Mindy's sister was a little more than distraught at the reception and she took it out on you. You were upset and went outside for some air. I followed to make sure you were okay and Charlie . . ." His eyes lowered before looking away in distraction. "He must have seen us in the parking lot because after you went back inside, he confronted me about it."

"He saw us?"

"Yeah," he replied with a small nod.

She saw the unsettled emotions he was trying to hide.

"He realized what . . . was going on and we got into it."

"What do you mean *you got into it*?"

"They fought, verbally and physically," Donna explained.

Rebecca saw Eric lower his eyes.

He rose from the bed and began to pace the small room. "You tried to plead with Charlie to listen, but he didn't want to hear it and then you collapsed."

"Oh God," she replied, running her hands through her hair in guilt, realizing she hadn't thought of Charlie since she'd woken up. Charlie's angered face flashed in her mind. "Have you talked to him?"

"I tried to explain, but he won't listen. He's still too angry."

"Maybe I should talk to him."

"Absolutely not."

"Why not?"

"It's not a good idea, Beccs," Donna added before she looked to Eric and they heard her phone ring. Donna pulled it out of her pocket and looked at it. "I have to take this." Donna rose from her seat and moved out of the room.

Rebecca felt unsettled and confused. Unsettled by what happened with Charlie and confused by Eric's reaction to her wanting to try to help. "Eric . . ."

His head fell back and his shoulders slumped. "This is not open for discussion, Beccs." His eyes were conflicted, but his face was determined. "You're not talking to Charlie. You don't need to be in the middle of this. He's my brother and I'll handle it."

"But I'm already in the middle."

"Okay, well, then I'm taking you out."

"Eric," she called, watching him pace. "If you don't want me to talk to Charlie, I won't." Rebecca reached out to pull him toward her and he sat on the bed. She lifted her hand to his scruffy cheek. She caressed it and he turned into it, kissing her palm. He leaned closer to her and she wrapped her arms around his neck, hugging him. His arms pulled her into him. His breath against her neck, she closed her eyes, wishing she could make him feel better. The situation was what they'd been trying to avoid all of these weeks and now there was nothing left but to hope for the best.

She loosened her grip on his neck, seeing his eyes heavy with emotion. His lips gently came down to hers and she drank in the sweetness of his kiss. He eased her back on the bed before he broke the embrace and looked down at her, a deep tenderness in his eyes.

"How are you feeling?" he asked, his fingers mingling in the folds of her hair.

She fought to hide a sudden wave of nausea pushing at the back of her throat. "I'm fine."

"Okay," he replied with a nod and a smirk, his thumb caressing her cheek. "So how about now you tell me the truth."

"I just . . ." She rolled her eyes, frustrated for being so weak. "My head hurts."

"Do you want me to call the nurse?" His face creased in concern.

Her eyes became heavy. "No, I would prefer to step away from drugs for the moment." The thudding of her head increased and she couldn't help but wince.

"Why don't you try to sleep," he suggested, stroking her

hair.

"Do you know how ridiculous that sounds? I just spent the last fifteen hours sleeping."

"I don't think it counts," he replied with a small grin, brushing her bottom lip with the tip of his finger. "Besides, if your body is telling you to rest, you should listen. We don't need you getting worse instead of better because you're being stubborn."

"Yeah because lying in a hospital bed is so strenuous. And I'm not stubborn."

"Okay," he replied, his mouth twitching in amusement.

"What is that supposed to mean?"

"Nothing."

"Tell me one time where I've been stubborn."

"Just one?"

"You're awful!"

"Who's awful?" Donna re-entered the room, seeing them laughing.

"Eric."

"I am not."

"He thinks I am stubborn and yet he can't come up with an example," she replied, raising her eye brow with a smirk.

His eyes grew with open amusement. "No, I was confirming you only needed one."

"Because there are so many to choose from," Donna added, simultaneously typing on her blackberry.

"There are not."

"Regardless, my point is, like it or not, you're going to need to take it easy for a few days until this passes."

"Not insisting you can do everything yourself," Donna added. "You're going to need to let us help, Beccs."

"Fine, but I'm not an invalid." She saw the objection to her statement on both of their lips. "There really isn't anything wrong with me. I'm just a little tired, but, if it will keep you two from hovering, I will relax for a few days and let you help."

"Thank you," Eric squeezed her hand and Donna smirked.

"Don't thank me yet," she said, looking to Eric. "So I have a favor to ask. "

"Anything."

"I'm hungry."

"Well that's a good sign. What are you hungry for?"

"Chili Cheese Fries."

"Chili cheese fries?"

"Yes."

"Seriously."

"Yes."

"Okay, if that's what you want."

She smiled and he brushed her cheek before planting a soft gentle kiss on her lips.

"I'll be back."

"I'll be waiting."

Eric left the hospital and was back in little over an hour. Chili cheese fries and a coke in hand, he opened the door and stopped, seeing Rebecca was asleep. Donna rose from her chair beside the bed and met him.

"Hey," Donna said, stepping out of the hospital room. "She fell asleep just after you left."

"Thank God," Eric replied with a shake of his head and a small sigh of relief.

"Did you call your dad?"

"Yeah he's on his way with Charlie," Eric replied with a deep breath, putting the food on the table next to the set of chairs in the hall. Just after he left, Donna texted him Charlie was asking to see Rebecca. After some debate, they decided, considering the situation, they needed to be careful.

Eric knew Charlie had every right to see Rebecca, but he was concerned about what may happen on both sides. He'd just convinced Rebecca not to talk to Charlie. Given the circumstances, a friendly *Hi, how are you feeling* was unlikely, and he wasn't sure Rebecca was ready to deal with anything more.

Despite her insistence she was fine, he wasn't convinced and neither was Donna. So the compromise was to have Harry go in with Charlie, ensuring things didn't get out of control.

"Okay, I have an errand to run. I'll be back," Donna said.

Eric watched her disappear down the hall. Eric heard screaming and realized it was coming from Rebecca's room. He pushed through the door and found her bed empty. He searched the room and found her huddled in the far corner, crying.

She leaned heavily against the wall, her knees pulled tightly into her chest

"Beccs," he said in a rushed breath, crossing the room. The IV tower was on the ground and blood dripped down her arm. She gasped for breath and Eric lowered himself in front of her. Desperate not to scare her and make things worse, he moved slowly. Her eyes still closed, her body trembled. He reached out, gently grazing her hair with his fingertips. "Beccs," he said in a low gentle tone. He continued caressing her hair and her eyes opened in hesitation.

She saw him. Her shoulders fell and her eyes softened.

He leaned forward, pulling her into his chest. He guided her hands to his shoulders and shifted his weight. She clung to him and he gathered her into his arms, lifting her off the floor. A group of several nurses waited, their eyes keenly watching his movement toward the bed. He tried to lay her down, but was stopped when a small whimper followed her hands refusing to release her grip on him.

"Beccs, you're okay. I'm not going to leave you, but you need to lay back, baby," he whispered into her hair. She shook in his arms and his heart ripped in helplessness. Eric continued to hold her until she loosened her grip on his neck.

She laid back into the bed, her eyes heavy and filled with a deafening anxiety. Once her head was on the pillow, he leaned over, brushing her hair away from her cheek in reassurance. "The nurses need to check on you. I'm not leaving, I'll be right here, okay?"

He watched her nod in hesitation and he kissed her forehead before he began to move. He let the medical team pass him, but remained conscious to stay within her sight.

The medical team worked and Eric dug his hands in his pockets, desperate to restrain the need to hold her. His gaze landed across the room and he realized he was staring at his brother. The look of shock and confusion on Charlie's face was hardening and Eric wondered how long he'd been standing there. Harry pulled on Charlie's arm and his brother looked at Rebecca before tearing his gaze away and exiting the room.

Eric was paralyzed and unable to deal with his own conflicted emotions. He was terrified about what was happening to Rebecca and angry that Charlie decided to pick that moment to show up. He didn't know whether to rip himself or his brother to shreds.

Eric didn't think Rebecca noticed his brother's presence and decided Charlie would need to wait. The nurses finished after what seemed like hours and he moved to her bedside.

"Hey, beautiful," he said, taking her hand in his.

She looked at him with heavy eyes. "I'm sorry." Her eyes filled with tears.

He leaned over, brushing them from her cheek. "There is

nothing to be sorry for, sweetheart," he replied, causing the flood of tears to continue.

"I'm stronger than this."

He watched her try to hold back the tears.

"I don't know what's . . ."

"Shhh . . . stop. Please don't do this to yourself, baby."

"Eric, I can't—"

"You need to rest," he insisted. He brushed her temple with his thumb and she struggled to keep her eyes open. "No matter what happens, I'll be right here. I'm not going anywhere, so just close your eyes and rest."

He continued to try and sooth her into slumber. He took in her angelic face, asking himself what he'd done to deserve such a beautiful resilient creature. She apologized for not being strong enough and yet he saw nothing but exquisite steel in her eyes.

The door opened and Eric turned to see the doctor who'd examined Rebecca just hours before enter the room. He shifted off the bed and managed to rise without disturbing her, before he met the doctor. "She just drifted off."

The doctor nodded, making a note in her chart.

"The nurse gave her a mild sedative with a neural inhibitor to suppress any dreams she may have," he explained. "She'll be asleep for a while."

"What's happening? Is this a side effect of the drug?"

"It is hard to say, but with any kind of stress, the brain adapts to protect itself, then tries to repair the damage during sleep," the doctor began to explain. "Do you know if she's been exposed any kind of severe trauma recently?"

"Ah, yeah. Without going into detail, she's definitely been through trauma recently."

"How long ago was this?"

"It's been going on for weeks," Eric replied, shaking his head. "Her . . . she was at a friend's funeral when this . . .

happened."

"I can't say for sure, but I would guess Ms. Gailen has been working very hard to suppress recent events in an effort to cope," the doctor explained. "The drug she was dosed with has weakened her internal mental defenses, hence flooding her mind with all of the trauma she's been suppressing."

"What do you recommend?"

"Physically she needs to recover from the stress the drug has put on her body. Her body will grow stronger and so will her mind. We will take care of it while she's here. Once she's released, you are going to have to keep an eye on it at home."

"Is there anything I can do?"

"Just be here when she needs you," the doctor replied. "It's really all any of us can do."

"Thank you, Doctor . . ."

"Raines," he replied with a smile, shaking Eric's hand. "I'm going to check over her vitals, if you want to get some air. I saw there are some people waiting outside if you'd like to give them an update on her condition."

"I don't—"

"I'll be here, and she's going to be sedated for a while," the doctor replied with a reassuring nod. "She won't even know you're gone."

"Okay, thanks." He glanced back at Rebecca before he stepped out of the room and into the hallway.

"What the hell is going on, Eric?" Charlie immediately demanded.

"How is she, son?" Harry asked.

"She's sleeping," Eric replied as he exhaled the breath he'd been holding.

"What happened in there?" Charlie asked in a hard demanding tone.

"She had a reaction to the drug," Eric explained, leaving the details of the reaction purposely vague. "She needs to rest and recover. Other than that, we just need to wait and see what happens."

"Donna said you caught the bastard who did this," Harry chimed in and Charlie looked away.

"Yeah, they have him downtown," Eric replied, digging his hands into his pockets. His mind filled with the sound of her screaming behind the door. "He's confessed to everything."

"Seems to be too little too late, don't you think," Charlie commented.

Eric chose to ignore him.

"Charlie . . ." Harry objected.

"What?" Charlie snapped.

Eric felt the bubbling of resentment toward his brother.

"It's the truth! If he would have caught the bastard sooner, she wouldn't even be here!"

"You're right, I didn't find him fast enough," Eric admitted, falling into the trap of self-loathing guilt. "This is my fault."

"No, it's not, Eric," Harry objected. "You did everything you could to find this asshole. This is not your fault. This is his fault. I know for a fact Rebecca wouldn't want you blaming yourself for any of this mess!"

"God forbid Detective Stiles take any responsibility for this disaster."

"What do you want from me, Charlie?"

"I want you to walk away before you hurt her even more than you already have," Charlie demanded. "You don't deserve her. You know it and I know it."

"Charlie, that's enough!" Harry scolded.

"You're going to use her and when you get bored, you're going to walk away, just like all the others."

"I told you, it's not like that, Charlie."

"The hell it's not! She's in there because you couldn't walk away! She's in there because of your arrogance. You're going to use her up and throw her away just like—"

"Listen to me, little brother," Eric stepped forward, getting in Charlie's face. His father used his shoulder to create a barrier between them. "I know you think you know what you're talking about, but you don't. So until you're ready—"

"I've seen you do it a million times before! She's the damsel in distress, you're the hero—"

"No."

"Charlie, stop . . ." Harry interjected again.

"She's vulnerable and hence in your eyes, an easy piece of ass!"

"You don't get it!"

"I don't get what? That you're a miserable son of a bitch who can't stand to see anyone happy?"

"I'm in love with her!"

"You bastard. You heartless bastard—"

"That's right I'm a bastard and I don't give a damn what you think! The only person I care about is behind that door!"

"You have no right!"

"Yes I do! So take your judgments and your anger somewhere else because they're not helping anyone, especially Rebecca!" Eric latched on to his brother's stony expression and pushed it back on him with an icy glare. He felt Harry's hand on his shoulder and he broke his rigid stance before he turned away from his brother. Eric forced himself to calm down and refocus. He saw his father's understanding expression waiting and Charlie disappeared.

"Dad, I—"

"Don't worry about it. He needed to be knocked down a few pegs," Harry offered, shaking his head. "How is she doing?"

"They uh . . ." Eric started, taking a deep breath. His father led him to a set of chairs in the hallway. "They sedated her, gave her something to keep her from dreaming so she can rest. When did you and Charlie . . ."

"It doesn't matter, how are you doing, son?"

"I don't know, Dad," Eric replied, wiping his hands over his face. "I just feel so helpless."

"I know you do. You and Rebecca are going to get through this," Harry said, placing a reassuring hand on his shoulder. "I brought you some clean clothes and your razor so you can get cleaned up while she's resting."

"Thanks," Eric replied, glancing at the bag on the floor in front of him.

"Tell you what, how about you get cleaned up and I will sit with Rebecca for a while," Harry offered. "She's asleep and if anything happens, I'll come get you."

"I—"

"Eric, I know your instinct is to push on despite your own needs, but you running yourself ragged is not going to help Rebecca. It's only going to exacerbate the situation."

Eric sighed.

"Look, if she sees you falling apart, she's going to worry about you instead of focusing on her recovery. If you don't want to do it for you, then do it for her."

"Okay." He picked up the bag and looked to his dad with a sigh.

Harry patted him on the back and they walked into Rebecca's room together. Eric hesitated for a moment when he reached the bathroom. He then decided he could shower and change in less than half an hour. He would be only a few feet away.

She would be fine.

Chapter Nine

The darkness was warm and she could feel herself lifting out of it. After a moment, there was light. She opened her eyes and saw Eric's smiling face looking down at her, his hand encircling hers.

"Hey, beautiful," he said, squeezing her hand.

"Hey." She tried to jumpstart her brain.

"How are you feeling?"

She took a mental inventory. "Better." She leaned back into the pillow, her head still feeling a little heavy. "How long have I been asleep?"

"A few hours."

"Why didn't you wake me?"

"Because you needed to sleep." He brushed a stray curl off her cheek.

"I swear it feels like that's all I've been doing," she said in mild irritation when she noticed his clean-shaven face and a pang of disappointment ebbed at her. She raised her hand to his cheek, tracing the line of his jaw with her fingertip. "You shaved."

"Dad brought by my razor and a clean set of clothes," he replied with a grin, looking confused by her reaction. "Don't look so disappointed."

"I'm not disappointed," she replied with a smirk, pulling her hand back. "I just kinda liked the scruff."

"Really?" He leaned into her with a small smile. Her arms wrapped around his neck. "Well I'll definitely take that into consideration the next time I go to shave."

"That's all I am asking."

He moved his mouth over hers, before devouring its softness. He broke the embrace and looked at her hesitancy.

"What's wrong?"

"Charlie's here," Eric said, wrapping his hands around hers. "He wants to see you."

"Okay."

"I don't want you to do this if you aren't—"

"I'm fine. I'm better than fine. I want to see Charlie."

"Okay, but there are going to be some rules," he replied, taking a breath. "Harry is going to chaperone. I need you to promise me if it's too much you're going to say something, Beccs. I don't want you pushing yourself and with everything going on with Charlie . . ."

"Eric, I'll be fine," she said, trying to reassure him, but she could tell he still wasn't convinced. "I promise it will be fine and if I can't handle it, I will say something."

"You're sure?"

"Yes."

"Okay," he replied with a nod. "I'm going to go get them. Do you need anything?"

"Something to drink would be nice."

"You got it," he replied before he got off the bed and headed to the door.

Rebecca lay back, enamored by his protective nature. Her thoughts drifted to the pending conversation with Charlie. She knew Eric wanted the visit to be short and sweet, but she felt like she owed his brother an explanation. This was her fault. If she would've just been honest about her feelings for him from the beginning, they could have avoided this whole mess.

She ran her fingers through her hair, wishing for a mirror and a hot shower. She cringed at the thought of her appearance. Before she had a chance to worry about it, the door opened and Harry walked into the room, followed by Charlie.

"Hey, there she is!" Harry greeted, enveloping her in a warm hug. "As beautiful as ever!"

"Thanks, Harry," she replied, a blush crept onto her cheeks.

"Beccs," Charlie moved toward her and gave her a tight hug. "I was so worried."

"I'm fine, Charlie."

He pulled back, digging his hands in his pockets.

"A little tired, but besides that, I'm doing great."

"Good," he replied, glancing at Harry.

"Charlie," she said, getting his attention back. "I'm so sorry for how this all happened."

"It's not your fault, Beccs. I just don't understand what went wrong," he replied, sitting down on the side of the bed. "Was it something I did? I thought we—"

"It has nothing to do with you, Charlie. Like I said in the car, I love you and I always will as my friend," she replied, trying to push through the resentment in his eyes.

"I know you think you're in love with him, Rebecca, but you don't—"

"Charlie, please don't do this."

He rose from the bed, pacing the room like an angry tiger. "I'm sorry, but I just can't . . . I can't accept you're choosing him over me."

"I am not choosing anything. Try to understand, what we had was wonderful, but it was never going to be more than it was, even before Eric."

"Why didn't you say something?"

"I tried to—"

"When?"

"Charlie—"

"What does he have that I don't, Beccs?"

"Nothing, Charlie."

Promise me if it is too much you are going to say something, Beccs . . .

"Why do you love him and not me?"

"Charlie, that's enough," Harry interjected, taking her hand in reassurance.

"I'm so sorry," she offered, seeing his tortured face. "I know I should've told you. I just . . . I just didn't want to hurt you. Neither of us did."

"So am I supposed to just thank you for leading me on? For letting me believe we stood a chance?" Charlie spouted. Harry released her hand to cross the room, putting himself in front of Charlie.

"I said that's enough, Charles."

"No it's not, Dad, I deserve to know the truth!"

"She told you the truth, son. You just don't want to hear it."

"That's bullshit!" Charlie exclaimed.

Rebecca's body lurched. The blood drained from her cheeks and she began to tremble. "Harry . . ." She tried to breathe and stop the spinning room.

"He did this, I know he's manipulating . . ."

Charlie's voice bounced in her head.

"Why are you defending . . ."

"Harry . . ."

"Beccs," Charlie said.

The room filled with gray and she felt a warm hand around hers.

"Go get your brother," Harry said in a steady voice. "Breathe. Just breathe, Rebecca, let it pass."

"Beccs, I . . ."

"Charlie, go!" Harry commanded in a restrained but frustrated tone.

Rebecca continued to focus on her breathing clinging to the warmth in her hand.

"That's right, just breathe, Rebecca. You're doing great."

The fog started to lift from her eyes and the room ceased to spin. She heard the door open and Harry smiled. She focused her eyes and took another breath.

"Hey, how's it going in here?" Eric asked. Harry released her hand and Eric took his place.

"Much better," Harry replied.

Rebecca leaned back into the pillow, her eyelids heavy. The door opened again and she shifted to see Charlie standing in the doorway, his face blank and staring.

He stepped into the room. "Beccs," he started moving toward the bed. "I just . . ."

"Charlie," Eric started to object.

She squeezed his hand to stop.

"I just wanted to say I'm sorry if I upset you. That was never my intention, I never wanted . . ."

"I know you didn't, Charlie," she replied with a small nod and he looked to Eric before he walked out of the room. Harry gave her a wink and a smile before he left the room.

"What happened?" Eric asked.

"It doesn't matter," she replied, reaching up to touch his cheek.

"I told you—"

"Eric, I'm fine," she replied with a smile and he relented. His eyes turned soft, running his fingers through the twists of her hair.

"How are you feeling?"

"Sleepy." She sunk down into her pillow.

She shifted onto her side, offering him a spot in the bed. He kicked off his shoes and lay down next to her. She turned into his chest, feeling his fingertips brushing through her hair.

Her eyes closed against his touch and he leaned forward, kissing her forehead. She curled into him, feeling the blankets being pulled up and around her. His arms gently wrapped around her and she reveled in his warmth. Her entire body melted and she drifted away into a deep slumber.

Rebecca opened her eyes to the bright starched walls of the room and she looked around. Empty. With a deep breath, she shifted onto her back and took a quick self-assessment.

After a mental inventory, she actually felt pretty good. She tested the waters of her equilibrium and sat up, so far so good. There was no dizziness or nausea and she spotted a robe hanging off the edge of the bed. She wrapped herself in it before pushing the blankets off her legs.

She eyed the armoire, knowing her purse was inside and found herself tempted to grab it. There were various reasons for wanting it, the top being to prove that she was fine. Then everyone would stop walking on eggshells around her like she was going to break.

Rebecca eased herself slowly off the bed. The cool linoleum beneath her feet, she tested her weight on her legs. She felt sturdy enough to push off the bed. She took a step forward, struggling with her balance, and then another. She found having to concentrate so hard on such a simple task utterly ridiculous. She took another step. Her head swam and she searched for something to grab.

"Rebecca."

She turned to look, her legs giving way beneath her. Scooped up into strong arms, she found herself pulled into Eric's deep eyes.

"What do you think you're doing there, red?"

"Getting my purse." Her mind swayed and she closed her eyes in frustration.

"And you thought this was a good idea because?" He walked her to the bed.

"I'm feeling better," she replied, annoyed with his coddling. "I was fine."

"Which is why you can barely keep your eyes open and your lovely face is completely devoid of color."

She laid back and he pulled the blanket up around her. "You're exaggerating."

"Okay."

"I want to go home," she said, closing her eyes, praying for her mind to settle.

"Soon, baby, soon," he said, his hand on her cheek.

She began to drift away.

"I promise."

Rebecca shifted, a hovering warmth around her, and she commanded her eyes to open. She took a breath and seeing Eric, she smiled.

"Hey, bright eyes," he said.

She focused on his voice.

"How are you feeling?"

Rebecca made herself move and amazingly, nothing ached or throbbed. She was still a little groggy, but her head had cleared and she felt like she'd just awoken from a good night's sleep. "Like I am sick of people asking me that," she replied with a grin. "Good and I think . . . I'm hungry."

"Well that is always a good sign. What are you hungry for?" he started and then stopped. "Wait, let me guess, chili cheese fries."

"You were paying attention, Stiles. I'm impressed . . ." she started when the door opened and a nurse walked into the room with a stack of towels.

"There's Sleeping Beauty and Prince Charming," she greeted, moving to the bed. "How are we feeling this afternoon?"

"Afternoon?"

"Yeah, honey, you slept the day away," the nurse replied with a wink. "But that is a good thing, trust me. Now I hate to butt in, however, Ms. Rebecca and I have some things to discuss."

"I guess that is my cue," Eric said with a smile before kissing her forehead. "I'll be back."

Chapter Ten

Eric returned forty-five minutes later, chili cheese fries once again in hand. He opened the door to her room and stopped. Two detectives he recognized from narcotics and Lug were standing on one side of her bed, Donna was standing on the other. "What's going on?"

"Apparently they arrived just after you left," Donna said, glaring at the men in irritation.

"Stiles, take a breath," Lug said.

Eric moved past him to Rebecca.

"They only have a few questions and then they'll be gone."

"What kind of questions? You told me this was an open and shut case," Eric said, placing the bag on the table by her bed.

"Eric, it's fine," Rebecca said, grasping his hand. "We're almost done."

"I am still waiting for an answer to my question," Eric repeated, looking at the narcotics officers who remained silent.

"Detective Stiles, we have some unanswered questions. We were hoping Ms. Gailen could help shed some light on the answers," one of the detectives responded. "And as she said, we're almost done."

Eric looked to Lug and then to Rebecca who nodded that she was fine. He then looked to Donna who sighed, but nodded.

"You've got ten minutes." Eric walked out of the room and a moment later, the door open and Lug stepped out.

"What the hell is going on?"

"I know, I'm sorry, I tried to stop them, but it came down from the top," Lug explained apologetically. "When we ran Marco's history, it sent up a flag. He's connected to the Rios Drug Cartel and there is an active DEA investigation."

"I still don't understand what it has to do with Rebecca," Eric replied in frustration. The last thing he wanted was her mixed up in some narcotics sting. "She doesn't know anything about the Rios Cartel, Lug! You have—"

"It's a formality, Stiles, you know that," Lugow reassured. "They put her statement on the books and she's in the clear. They'll leave her alone."

Eric nodded in agreement, looking at his watch. "They have five more minutes and then I want them out of here. She's supposed to be resting," Eric said, restraining his fury against the situation.

"Five minutes and they're gone," Lug replied with a nod before he turned back to the room.

Eric scratched the back of his head, willing his heart to calm. He didn't like that this was happening and he didn't like that they showed up when he wasn't here.

He paced the floor, keeping a close eye on his watch. The door of Rebecca's room opened and Lugow escorted the two narcotics detectives down the hall.

Donna passed him on her phone and he stepped into the room. Eric found Rebecca chewing on her thumb. She sat upright while he moved toward the bed.

"Why were they asking about Marco?"

"Beccs, I—"

"Is he under some kind of investigation?"

"We're not talking about this."

"Why not?"

"Because we aren't."

"But what if I know something, Eric?"

"You don't."

"How do you know?"

"Enough," he said, pushing her food toward her. She took it from him with a glare he decided to ignore.

"If I don't know anything, then why are they questioning me about him?"

"Rebecca . . ." he replied in frustration, cursing the idiots who started this, and rose from the bed.

"Marco Valnes is a drug dealer," she said.

He silently continued to curse his job.

"I know that. I was in his house. I followed him around for over a week—"

"Stop, Beccs, Stop." He turned and saw the worry in her eyes. "Listen to me. This is not your problem. You've been through enough."

"He's the reason Lucy's in the hospital."

He walked back to the bed, meeting her eyes.

"She was a prisoner in his house. I had to literally carry her out because when I found her, she was higher than a kite, half-naked and slumped over a toilet! So if there is anything I can do to get a little justice for Lucy, or prevent it from happening to someone else, I want to do it."

"Okay, fine," he said, relenting. "I'll talk to Lug and let him know if they need anything else, within reason, they can ask."

"Thank you," she replied with a small smile.

The door opened and Dr. Raines entered the room to give them the good news of her release. The doctor went through the rules and the options, including a prescription for sleeping pills if she needed them. She nodded and agreed to all of them. Although Eric guessed, she would have agreed to leave a kidney behind if they would just allow her to go home.

It wasn't until after eight PM when they were in the truck and on their way home. She was quiet during the ride and he knew she had a lot on her mind. He had a surprise for her and he hoped it would lighten the load a little. It had taken a lot of help and almost a miracle, but he had pulled it off, now he just had to show her. "Do you trust me?"

"What?"

"Do you trust me?"

"Of course I trust you," she replied with a laugh.

"Okay, I want you to close your eyes."

She looked at him in disbelief.

"Close your eyes."

"Fine," she said.

He watched her close her eyes. They were a few blocks away and he hoped she hadn't been paying attention to their location or she may have already figured it out. "Keep them closed."

"Are we almost done?"

"Almost." He pulled in front of her house and parked the truck. "Keep your eyes closed and don't move."

"You're crazy."

He got out of the truck and closed the door. He pulled out her keys and unlocked the door. Once inside, he punched in the alarm code and glanced to see her waiting for him. He jogged back out and opened her door, hearing her giggle.

"What are you doing?"

"Keep them closed." He helped her out of the truck and then scooped her into his arms.

"What are you doing? I can walk, you know!"

"I'm not taking any chances. Keep your eyes closed."

"They are closed already," she replied, covering her eyes with her hands.

Eric carried her across the lawn and through the door. He put her on her feet, standing behind her. He wrapped his hands around hers, praying this would work, and took a breath. "Okay, open them," he said, pulling her hands away from her eyes.

She looked around the room and then took a deep breath.

Eric had called in a lot of favors, his dad, Donna, Adam, Lug, Misty, Mike, Don, Jerry and anyone else he could think of. They all came in and removed any trace of the grotesque display covering her walls. They repainted everything, had a cleaner come in, wipe everything down and even bought her a new couch. It was a huge undertaking, but he'd managed to pull it off.

When she didn't say anything, he began to worry. "Beccs?" He moved to look at her. "Are you okay?"

She turned to face him. Tears in her eyes, she looked up with a quivering smile. She wrapped her arms around him.

He heard a broken thank you against his neck. "You're welcome," he replied with a small sigh of relief.

"How did you do this?" She looked up at him in disbelief.

"I told you, I have connections."

"But, Eric, you . . ."

"You said you wanted to go home," he said, holding her face in his hands. He felt her raise herself to her toes. He leaned down, touching her lips against his with a tender adoration. He tried to tell her without words how much she meant to him. He tasted her tears and, lifting his mouth, brushed away the wetness with his thumb. "No more tears."

She nodded in agreement.

Eric released her and let her take it in. He went to the truck and grabbed her things. Back within moments, he closed the door, seeing her in the kitchen. "Are you hungry? I can run and get you something if you want," he asked, putting her bag on the floor by the door.

"No, I'm just looking for something to drink. Darn it, I'm out of cream," she said, pulling water from the fridge. "Do you want something?"

"I'll take water." He walked into the kitchen and she handed him a bottle of water. "Feel good to be home?"

"You have no idea." She took a sip of her water and then looked away from him, her eyes becoming dark. "Do you really think it's over?"

"Rebecca . . ." he started moving toward her, the question shaking him.

"I want the truth." Her eyes shone in hesitant desperation.

He wrapped his hand around hers, pulling her toward him.

"I don't want you to protect me, Eric. I want you to tell me the truth. Is this really over?"

"Yes," he said, meeting her eyes. "The man who did all of this is sitting in a dark jail cell, where he will be for a very long time. He's not coming back, it's over."

"Eric—"

"Listen to me, you're home." She tried to object and he tangled his hands in her hair. "I am here and you're safe, Beccs. I promise. There's nothing for you to be afraid of anymore." He watched her nod, but looked for any sign of doubt in her eyes. Seeing none, he gathered her into his arms, holding her against him. "It's getting late," he said, looking down into her tired eyes. "And you need to sleep."

She nodded.

He turned her around in his arms and walked her toward the bedroom. Kissing her head, he released her to go get changed and grabbed the familiar duffel bag Harry had left by the door. Digging through it, he pulled out a pair of boxers and a t-shirt. He stripped down and changed.

Rebecca appeared from the bathroom a few minutes later. She pulled down the blankets on the bed. Her beautiful hair up in a ponytail, a plain white t-shirt and blue shorts covered her small frame. Eric walked through the house, turned off the lights, checked the doors and armed the alarm. She sat in bed, waiting for him. She reached over and turned out the light and he climbed in next to her. She curled into him and he wrapped his arms around her. Comfortable in each other's embrace, they drifted off together.

CHAPTER ELEVEN

"Tell me you want me," his rough voice breathed into her ear and she squared her shoulders in defiance. She struggled against him, her clothes ripping away from her body . . .

"No!" *she screamed and broke away.*

She pushed her feet forward, tearing through the trees and shrubs blocking her path. She could feel him pounding behind her. She saw a light ahead. Rushing through the foliage, she reached the door, yanking it open. She fled down the corridor, looking for somewhere to hide.

She could hear the echoing of his shoes off the walls. Seeing a double door at the end of the long hall, she ran toward it, pulling on the handle. It wouldn't budge and she panicked, hearing his approach.

All at once, the door released and she pulled it back. Met with the sight of blood, decay and needless violence, Beccs's body and spirit revolted against it. She doubled over in anguish at the horrid sight, backing out of the room. She felt someone behind her and spinning around, she met faceless cold dark eyes. Covered in blood, smiling viciously at her, he reached forward grabbing her by the neck and squeezing.

"Hello, Beccs!"

She jerked awake, her body rigid. She blinked and sat upright, her body melting in fear. She focused her eyes to see Eric lying next to her. Her mind screamed in agony and she fought to regain control.

It's over. You need to let it go . . .

She lifted off the bed. Desperate not to wake him, she padded across the room and slipped out of the bedroom. She walked to the fridge, flipping on the small light above the sink, then she grabbed a water. She stared blankly at nothing, her mind still exhausted and begging for renewal. She shook herself out of the trance before she walked into the living room, still in awe of what he'd done.

She was sure the blood would never come off and her house was in essence ruined. When she opened her eyes and saw what he'd done, she was so overwhelmed she thought she was going to faint. Instead she cried, which was an embarrassment in itself.

She smiled and took a seat, becoming absorbed by the pillows of her new couch. She turned on the TV in search of something to watch. Cartoons were always entertaining so she stopped on The Cartoon Network and just let her mind be preoccupied with silliness for a while.

She fought the heaviness of her eyes, fearing what laid in wait on the other side. Not having the energy to sustain the battle, she slipped into sleep.

She was warm and comfortable, safe.

Feeling a drip of water fall on her cheek, she brushed it away without thought, falling back into the warmth of her soft cocoon. Feeling it again, she wiped it away and then feeling it again, she wiped it away and opened her eyes. Sitting up, feeling an overwhelming grogginess, she felt another drip, hearing it touch her cheek. Wiping it off her cheek again, she looked at her hand and saw blood. The droplets continued, becoming a rain of blood on her and looking up in confusion, saw Eric's eyes wide and cold, his bloodied body hung from the ceiling, dripping down on her.

Rebecca screamed.

Just once, he'd like to wake up and find her next to him, sleeping. He was determined it would happen, outside of a hospital bed. Eric rolled out of bed, looked at the time and wondered how long she'd been awake.

It was a little after nine-thirty and scratching the back of his head, he smelled coffee. He found her against the kitchen counter, coffee in hand, reading a magazine. "Morning," he said, making his way to the coffee, a cup waiting for him.

"Morning," she replied, looking at him with a bright smile. "How did you sleep?"

"Fine." He walked to the fridge for cream. "How about you?"

"Good." Not looking up from the magazine, she took a sip of her coffee. "It felt good to be back in my own bed."

"I can imagine." He walked the cream back to the counter where his cup was waiting. "How long have you been up?"

"Ummm . . . not long," she replied, discarding the magazine to the counter and met his eyes. "I'm going to jump in the shower."

He took a sip of coffee and leaned on the counter while he debated whether he wanted to push her on the topic. She disappeared into the bedroom and he scanned the house, looking for any clues to support his suspicion.

He noticed the mail was missing from the table, but she could've gone through it in a short amount of time. Laundry basket on top of the dryer was new, but again she could've done it in the time before he got out of bed.

Then he saw her car keys on the counter and his stomach tightened. He picked them up, searching his mind for a reason she would've left. He took a sip of his coffee and then remembered her mentioning she didn't have any cream.

He dropped the keys and went to the garbage can. A plastic bag from the local corner market sat on top and he pulled it out. Not only did he find the receipt, he also saw two used coffee-filled filters. He unfolded the receipt—the time of purchase was 3:36 AM.

Jesus, Beccs . . .

He needed to think about this. Yes, she'd been up since close to 3 AM and she'd taken her car to go get cream. However, it was just down the street and there wasn't a problem or he would've known it.

Maybe she couldn't sleep. It was likely considering how much sleep she'd been getting. He didn't want to make a big deal about it, despite his concerns. He'd keep an eye on her and take it a moment at a time. It was the best decision for now. He knew if he tried to confront her about it, she'd just deny it or get angry with him for trying to control her which wasn't productive either.

She needed to rest and relax.

He did his best to let it go and half an hour later, she emerged from the bedroom, looking refreshed and smiling.

"I saved you some hot water," she said, pouring herself a fresh cup of coffee.

"Thanks." He rose from the couch, shuffling into the bedroom for his turn in the bathroom. He showered, changed and walked out of the bathroom to find her making the bed. He walked up behind her, encircling her waist. His breath slid across her neck before he caressed the delicate skin with his lips and she giggled. She turned into his chest with a smile before tousling his still damp hair.

"So are you all squeaky clean?"

"I don't know about squeaky, but I've gotten rid of my morning breath." He pulled her against him.

"Really." She titled her head in disbelief. "Maybe I should make sure, just to be safe."

"I think I can handle that . . ." he started, his words disappearing with the touch of her soft, tantalizing lips. She wrapped her arms around his waist and he smoothed the hair off her face as their lips parted. "So, how about we take a trip and get some movies for the day. Then you and I can sit on the couch and veg out for a while?"

"Okay," she replied with a small nod.

"Yeah?"

"Yeah, that sounds nice."

"Okay, grab your shoes and we'll take off."

She gave him a quick kiss before she walked away. Pleasantly surprised by her reaction to the suggestion, within a few minutes, they headed out to the truck and off to the video store.

Eric let her take her pick of movies. He wasn't disappointed, seeing more than one in the stack he'd wanted to watch. He'd assumed he was going to have to endure a plethora of chick flicks, thankfully he was wrong.

They grabbed some snacks and sodas, checked out and then headed back to the house. When they returned, she went into the kitchen and began washing out the coffeepot and cups. He was about to object when his phone rang and he saw Harry's number. "Hey, Dad."

"Hey, just wanted to check in and see how you guys were doing."

"We're good."

She glanced back at him while she dried her hands.

"Just picked up some movies and getting ready to settle in on the couch."

"Is Rebecca feeling better?"

"Yeah, she's doing well. Have you seen Charlie at all?"

"No, and I don't want you to worry about it, Eric. You need to focus on Rebecca. Your brother needs to cool off. Space and time are the best things for both of you right now."

"Yeah okay, thanks, Dad," he replied with a small sigh. "Talk to you later."

Harry bid him farewell and Eric laid the phone on the counter. He saw it was almost one and realized she hadn't eaten yet. He mentally kicked himself for not picking something up on the way home.

"So how's your Dad?"

"Fine, just checking in." He leaned against the counter, phone back in hand. "So I'm starving, what are you in the mood for?"

"I don't care, whatever."

"Okay you can't do that, not yet anyway. Unless you want to eat chili cheese fries forever . . . you need to at least give me a hint."

"Okay . . . although now that you mention it . . ."

He wrapped his arms around her and she leaned into his chest. "Beccs . . ."

"Okay, seriously, I am game for anything but Chinese."

"Dominic's it is." He dialed the phone, her cheek resting against his chest. He hung up the phone after placing their order and leaned down to kiss the top of her head. "Pizza will be ready in about twenty minutes. Do you want to come with me to get it?"

"No, I think I'm going to stay here. I need to go through and delete some crap off the DVR."

"So I can assume you're going to be sitting on the couch when I leave and when I return?"

"Yep," she replied with a nod.

He looked down at her with a smile.

"Oh . . . crap . . ."

"What?"

"I told Donna I'd call her," she said, searching for her phone.

He waited until she looked up at him in mild irritation.

"Can I have my phone please?"

He'd confiscated it just before they left the hospital when he caught her trying to check her email. "Yes, but only to call Donna," he replied with a nod, releasing her and walking into the bedroom.

"Eric . . ."

"One phone call, no voicemail and absolutely no email."

He returned and trapped her against the counter.

"Because it takes so much energy to listen to a few voicemails."

"It does when you start getting stressed out about them and forget that part of resting is relaxing."

"Fine."

"What?"

"Fine," she replied.

"Promise me."

"Eric . . ."

"Promise," he gave giving her a stern look telling her he wasn't going to relent.

"I promise to be good," she said with a sigh.

He smirked before handing her the phone. "I'm going to get our food." She began dialing the phone and he kissed her forehead. "Be good."

"Blah, blah, blah."

He laughed, grabbed his keys and left the house.

CHAPTER TWELVE

Rebecca smiled and hung up the phone, happy to have talked to Donna. The conversation was light and she promised to rescue her from Eric tomorrow. Not that he hadn't been wonderful, but she missed her friend.

She rose from the couch, grabbed a water from the fridge and a stack of paper plates from the cupboard for the pizza. Dominic's, while tasty, was greasy so they'd also need paper towels. She reached to the top of the fridge to grab them when everything around her went gray.

She tried to blink it away, but it only got worse and her legs melted beneath her. She gripped the counter in an attempt to control her descent. She found herself sitting on the floor, her head feeling like a weighted anchor. She closed her eyes and leaned against the cabinet. She focused on her breathing, wishing the gray sloshing in her head to go away.

Somewhere in the distance, she heard the sound of a door closing and someone said her name. She opened her eyes and saw Eric crouched in front of her.

"Rebecca."

She took a deep breath, feeling the fog in her eyes begging them to close.

"Hey, red, how about we get you to the couch?"

She nodded, willing her limbs to move, feeling him lift her into his arms. She laid a weary cheek on his shoulder. When she opened her eyes again, she was laying on the couch with him looking down at her in concern.

"I can't leave you alone for ten minutes," he commented,

his fingers stroking her temple.

"Sure you can, just make sure it's in a padded room," she replied, making him smile and letting out a small laugh.

"What happened?"

"I was getting paper towels and everything got fuzzy."

He handed her a bottle of water. "I guess my idea about you sitting on the couch while I was gone wasn't very realistic, huh?"

"Hey, you said my butt needed to be on the couch when you left and again when you returned. You said nothing about the time between."

"And you were surprised I chose a lawyer," he replied, shaking his head at her with a grin.

"I'm sorry," she said, reaching out to caress his face. "I didn't mean to—"

"I know you didn't," he turned into her hand, kissing the palm. "But this does mean you're not allowed to do any more running around. You need to rest and I haven't seen you sit down since we got up this morning."

"I—"

"Don't even try it," he objected, giving her a stern look of warning. "This is not up for negotiation, okay?"

"Okay." Not having the energy to fight him. "Did you get pizza?"

"Yep, Dom even sent some cannoli's for you, on the house. He said he's hoping you feel better."

"And how, exactly, did Dom know I wasn't feeling well?"

"Well I got quizzed as to why I ordered a veggie delight pizza. Mike must've said something to him about what happened at the funeral because he asked how you were."

She flipped through the channels, sinking into the couch

"Great, so what you're telling me is all of Las Vegas knows."

"Pretty much." He joined her on the couch with two

plates of pizza and only one soda.

"Where's my soda?"

"You drink your water first and then you can have a soda," he said, handing her the plate.

"Oh, you're in so much trouble."

"You can beat me up all you want when you're feeling better."

She kicked him in the hip.

He swayed a little and then looked at her.

She suppressed a smile.

"Behave."

"No," she replied, unable to suppress the giggle bubbling from her chest.

"Keep it up, red," he commented back, taking a bite of his pizza. "So what are we watching?"

"I recorded something on the history channel I thought you would appreciate," she replied, switching to her DVR, choosing a two-hour special on the Sphinx.

"Is this the one where they — "

"Uh-huh."

"Sweet!"

They finished their pizza while watching their two-hour special. When it finished, they decided to go with a drama from the video store. This was followed by a comedy and finished with another special on Egypt. By this time, they were laying on the couch together. Eric lay on his side against the back of the couch while she lay in front of him. Her head rested in the crook of his shoulder, his arm draped around her waist.

They reached the first half hour of the special on the kings and queens of Egypt and her eyelids became heavy. She began to drift off. Fighting against it to no avail, she let herself fall into his encompassing warmth, slipping into slumber.

She was walking through The Rustic looking for something. The crowd was thick and she struggled to push through them, an unknown urgency in her chest. She saw a man with a gun walk into the back of the bar. No one could hear her over the roar of the crowd. She tried to call out, and pushing her way through, caught sight of someone familiar. Charlie was walking across the far end of the bar. Following him with her gaze, he met with Mindy. She saw Donna approach them both.

She looked back to the door and couldn't find the gunman. Panicking, she searched for him, the crowd broke and she couldn't find him anywhere. Turning, she saw Harry and Eric talking. Eric met her eyes and started walking toward her with a broad smile. She heard a shot and Harry's chest exploded before he fell forward. She watched Charlie fall. She heard another pop and then another when Donna fell. Mindy screamed in horror, her hands and face covered in blood. Rebecca begged her feet to move. She looked to Eric before she tried to run to him. Another pop echoed against her heart. He stopped, his eyes dropped and he looked down. She followed his eyes, his shirt spreading with blood. He fell, she saw the gunman standing just behind him, laughing at her, and she screamed.

Her eyes began to get heavy a quarter of the way through the show and he watched her fight it off. He knew her body would win and it did. She'd been asleep for about an hour and he'd finished the Egyptian special before he turned it to SportsCenter. It was ending when he felt her shift. At a glance, she seemed fine.

Eric began flipping through the channels. He looked for something to watch, and felt her shift again. Within a breath, she screamed and sat upright on the couch. It took a moment for him to catch up. She curled into herself, her body shaking. "Beccs," he said, wrapping his arms around her. She turned into his chest, still trying to catch her breath. He held her against him and her body began to still. She looked up at him, her eyes shadowed by the terrifying dream. "Are you okay?"

She nodded, taking in a deep breath.

He kept her within his arms and leaned back into the couch. She lay against his chest and he let her focus on the TV

She'd scared the shit out of him and he wondered if she felt his heart racing. One minute she was sleeping and the next she was trembling in his arms.

It was just before ten and he wondered how difficult it was going to be to get her to go to bed sooner rather than later. They settled on a string of Bugs Bunny cartoons. After about an hour, he could feel her breathing deepen.

He stroked her hair and another hour went by before he felt comfortable enough to close his eyes. With her safe in his arms, he drifted off. He felt her tremble against him and his eyes opened. His hand went into her hair, brushing her forehead with a kiss.

"You're okay, I'm right here, baby," he whispered into her ear. Her trembling seemed to stop and she relaxed again. He rested his cheek on her forehead, rethinking what he'd found that morning.

She was up before 3 AM. Had she had a nightmare? How could he have not realized it? She got out of bed without him noticing. She could've woken up long before and he'd never known.

He didn't know what to do and his heart ached. Eric remembered what the doctor had said at the hospital. If this continued, he was going to need to find a way to convince her to take the sleeping pills. He filled the prescription before they left the hospital and they were waiting in her bag.

Eric hoped he was just getting ahead of himself. He tried to remain optimistic. After all, she'd only had one nightmare so far. He glanced down at her now peaceful face and hoped to God it was her last. He shifted, pulling her a little closer, and started to feel the call of slumber.

He felt her shift against him. He wasn't sure how long they had been asleep. He began to stroke her hair, hoping he could calm her again. Without warning, she exploded into a ball of quivering fury. She pushed against him and he struggled to wake her.

"Beccs, stop, you're okay . . ." She continued to pound against him and he grasped her arms. "Beccs, it's me."

Her eyes cleared, looking at him in confused shock. She pushed her hand through her hair and attempted to take a breath. It came out broken and shaken.

"Beccs." He leaned toward her and she refused to meet his eyes. "It's okay." He brushed her cheek with his thumb and she met his gaze. Her eyes revealed her desperation to remain in control. She blinked and a tear fell down her cheek. Despite her own defiance, she wrapped her arms around his neck. He took a breath, caressing her hair.

He was reluctant to let her go when she moved off him and into the kitchen. He followed, finding her against the counter, staring down at a bottle of water. Eric waited for her to say something and then decided it was time. He walked into the bedroom, retrieving the bottle of sleeping pills. He returned to the kitchen and placed them on the counter next to her hand.

"It's time for bed. Baby, you need to sleep." She tried to look at him in irritation, but failed out of pure exhaustion. "You can't keep going like this. I know you don't want to, but I'm here and nothing is going to happen."

"Eric . . ." she started, her eyes brimming with tears, the hesitation and fear shining back at him.

"Please, please trust me," he begged, his fingers running through her hair. He watched her blink back the tears of uncertainty and take a deep breath. Eric wiped the tears from her cheek before he grabbed the bottle of pills and poured two into her hand.

She drank them down with her water, still looking like a terrified child. He wrapped his arms around her shoulders and walked her into the bedroom. They both changed and crawled into bed. She lay on her back and he slid in beside her. Her eyes stared up at the ceiling. Eric rolled onto his side, tracing the line of her hair with his fingertip. She looked at him with tentative but loving eyes. He reached for her and she turned into his chest. He felt her take a deep shaken breath and he kissed the top of her head.

Eric waited for her to fall asleep before relaxing. He knew the pills were doing their job and began to drift off.

He bolted up out of a dead sleep, her desperate screams echoing in his mind. Eric saw her sitting up right beside him. She continued to scream, her hands wrapped around her neck. He scrambled around to face her, cupping her face as she sobbed. "Rebecca, baby, wake up," he begged, seeing her eyes were still closed.

"*No!*" she screamed, swinging at his arms, trying to escape from whatever was hurting her in the dream. "*You bastard!*"

"Beccs, you're safe, sweetheart. It's just a dream," Eric said, trying to cut through her terrified screams.

She gasped and collapsed back into the bed.

He watched her curl into a ball and cry in agony. He touched her cheek, laying alongside her, and she open her eyes.

They were weary and red, searching his, and then the fog seemed to lift.

"Eric . . ." she said, her hand clutching his wrist. I can't . . ."

"Shhh . . . you're okay." she tried to sit up and he shifted, letting her rest against him. "You're okay, it's over."

She clung to him and he moved her down with him, resting back into the bed. She rounded her body to fit in his embrace. He pulled the blankets around her small form, her head resting in the area between his head and shoulder. He stroked her hair and felt her begin to relax. It was going to be a long night.

Eric lay holding her, having resolved not to sleep. His senses attuned to her every movement, noise and breath. After two hours, she seemed to fall into a deep sleep and he released her from his embrace. She lay back into the pillows without notice and he rose from the bed, walking into the living room.

He went straight to his phone and digging in his wallet, pulled out Dr. Raines's business card. He reached the doctor's messaging service and asked to have him call back. Eric pulled out a bottle of water in frustration. Taking a drink, he leaned against the counter.

If she woke up again, he wasn't sure what he was going to do. The sleeping pills were supposed to help. They didn't, however, help to curb the intensity of the dreams. He refused to think about what she was dreaming. The possible images burned his mind enough without focus. He couldn't imagine what they were like in her own mind. She'd been through so much and suppressed all of it just to survive. Now her mind had revolted, demanding she face the buried fear, whether she was able to or not.

He'd had his share of nightmares over the years. Unconscious fears of his life falling apart, rearing their ugly head. Nothing like this.

He returned to the darkened room. His body was tired and ached, but his mind stayed alert with a mixture of worry and anticipation. He prayed she'd stay asleep, having sweet calming dreams. He watched her curved body relaxed in slumber and shivered, knowing it would be inevitably broken by the apparent terror of her mind.

Eric took his spot next her, continuing to watch her and despite himself, he drifted off. The sound of her crying pulled him from the hovering darkness. He reached for her and she rolled into his embrace, her chest heaving in anguish. "Hey, hey," he wrapped his arms around her, kissing her forehead. "It's okay, baby."

"He won't leave me alone," she admitted into his chest.

He released a long breath.

"Every time I close my eyes, he's there . . . and I just . . . I'm so tired . . ."

Eric woke on the couch. He felt her hands in his hair, his head resting on her legs. He shifted onto his back. He glanced to the clock. It was after ten. She was watching the television, her head resting on the arm of the couch.

He remembered her having several more nightmares when her stubborn nature kicked in. He followed her out to the living room to watch TV. The hope being if distracted by the mindless entertainment she would finally sleep.

Apparently not.

He lifted himself into a sitting position and reached out, brushing her hair with his fingertips. She met his eyes before she crawled into his lap. He held her against him and she curled against his chest.

"We're going to get through this, Beccs. I promise."

Chapter Thirteen

She crawled off his lap and back to the arm of the couch. He rose and grabbed his phone. She heard him leaving a message for Dr. Raines. The pills hadn't helped. If anything, they seemed to extend the torture of the visions. The nightmares seemed to cling and she struggled to break free. So now, she didn't close her eyes at all. The threat of images behind her eyes was more persuasive than the call of slumber.

She didn't remember when Donna arrived. Harry appeared out of nowhere. He sat next to her on the couch and she decided she'd lost her mind.

Rebecca half-heard everything said to her or around her. She remembered Eric and some pills before a warm blackness she couldn't escape wrapped around her mind. She tried to struggle despite her mind's warning and then she was floating weightless in a liquid of light.

She opened her eyes and found herself in her own bed, enveloped in comfortable sunshine. Her mind was light and she took a deep cleansing breath. She rolled onto her back, feeling him next to her. Sound asleep, she smiled at his calm face before reaching out to run her fingers over the scruff of his chin. She watched him shift and then he opened his eyes. He instantly looked down at her in concern and she smiled at him.

"She wakes." His hand wrapped in her hair.

"How long have I been asleep?"

"Depending on what time it is, about a day or so."

"A day! Are you kidding me? Eric—" He leaned forward, silencing her with a kiss.

"Do you feel better?"

"Yes."

"Then it doesn't matter." His lips teased her with a grin.

She lifted herself against him, seizing his lips. Curling her fingers in his hair, her body tingled. His mouth explored and she wanted more.

He enfolded her within his arms and she met his gaze. It was like a soft caress, but there was a hint of hesitation. She drew his face to hers in a renewed embrace, quivering at the sweet tenderness of his kiss.

Long drugging kisses within his arms sparked the flames of desire and they started to roll forth, pooling into her stomach, waiting to be ignited. She made a trail up his back with the edges of her nails and pulled at his shirt. He groaned before breaking their kiss to yank off his shirt. His heated lips and body pressed against her, his fingers pushing into her hair. She explored the hard planes of his back and shoulders with her fingertips. He devoured her lips and tongue before trailing down her cheek to the side of her neck. His warm mouth sucked and nipped, sending shivers up her spine and tingles to her core.

His hands pushed beneath her t-shirt. His soft hand caressed her skin. Moving up, his thumb teased her tender nipple, sending bursts of lightning through her body. He tugged her shirt up and over her head and then his mouth closed over the enflamed nipple. She arched in response, a delicious fire pulsing through her body. He suckled and she whimpered in wanting delight. Her hips lifted against him, feeling his already steel cock within his boxers.

He continued to suckle and tease her nipples, alternating back and forth. The throbbing ache rose through her body and his hand grazed her flesh. He lingered at the swell of her hip with light caresses. She hovered in torturous anticipation, lifting her hips against his hand in want. His mouth on her nipples was unrelenting. Electric bursts of fire shot through her body. She became desperate, in need of more of him.

His hand slipped beneath her shorts into her panties. He stroked her pussy, teasing her with anticipation and she squirmed against him. She dug her nails into his shoulder, his suckling of her breast tightening. She felt a slight pressure on her clit and her entire body tightened. The pressure slowly increased and she felt the heat of his breath on her neck just before he slipped two fingers into her. He wasted no time, going straight to her g-spot. Her body exploded and she arched off the bed in a cry of delight. He tugged at her lips and then disappeared.

Breathless at the way he was able to play her body, her nerves continued to scream for his tender attention. She felt him shift, his hands tugged on her hips, pulling off her shorts. He discarded the last of his clothing and she lifted herself up onto her knees, waiting for him. His eyes devouring her, he kneeled on the bed, moving toward her.

"You're so goddamn beautiful," he said in a strained voice.

His hands folded into her hair, pulling her head back. His heated body pressed against her, his mouth claiming her neck. His tongue tortured the sensitive nerves and she panted within the fire. The smooth lines of his body beneath her hands, she made a path across his shoulders and back before she reached between them. Her hand encircled his hardened cock. She felt him nip at her neck, her slow caress teasing him. She stroked him before cupping his balls, grazing them with her fingernails. His heaviness resting in her hand, she continued to use her grip to torture him. Her fondling intensified and his cock hardened. She remembered the feel of him throbbing within her body and a shiver of intense longing tightened within her cunt. She squeezed him at the base. His hands clenched the muscles of her lower back before a guttural moan erupted from his chest.

"Are you trying to kill me?"

She couldn't suppress her smile. He lifted the wrist of her devilish hand onto his shoulder. His arm braced her back, his free hand supporting her neck. He controlled her descent onto the bed. His hard body singed her, his mouth once again teasing her nipple with his tongue. The swelling need in her stomach ached for him. She pulsed with every heartbeat and her impatience grew to explosive proportions. She scraped her nails up his back and shoulders, a desperate cry for release escaping her lips. His tongue traced its way down her enflamed body. She panted uncontrolled, her body screaming she was unable to focus on any one thing.

He attached his mouth to her clit while pushing two fingers against the inside of her cunt. He teased the spot he knew made her scream, his tongue and fingers creating waves of ecstasy to crash through her body. She became lost in the swelling heat, her hips moved of their own accord. His tongue fiercely teased her clit, pushing her up to the point of explosion and then leveling her back down with a calm slow stroke. He wound her up several times and finally her body revolted against his control. She felt her body pound with each heartbeat.

"Eric . . . oh God . . . Eric!"

Her entire being erupted. His teasing focused, heightening the peaks of her pleasure. Her body continued to ripple when he released her. He captured her lips, cradling her in his arms. He raised her hips and with one smooth motion, his steel cock filled her, setting her body ablaze again with desire. Her body clutched his hard cock and she could feel every vein of his body within her. He smothered her lips with a soulful tender passion, capturing her gasp of utter delight.

The embrace was intimate, the strength of his arms shielding her from the world. She reveled in the closeness, his lips made unspoken promises. Her heart sighed in contentment. She breathed him in and melted, letting him consume her.

He began to move, his cock easily sliding in and out of her cunt. The thrusts were slow and controlled and she rolled her hips beneath him. His arms braced her back, lifting her against him. He remained inside her, shifting into a kneeling position. She wrapped her legs around him, her arms resting on his shoulders. She framed his face with her hands staring down into his eyes.

She kissed him passionately, riding his cock hard and slow. His hands gripped her hips, helping to control her movement. After a moment, he took back control, thrusting into her with a renewed fervor. The glorious assault had her gasping for air and she arched her back. His mouth latched on to her nipple. Her hands dug into his hair, searching for an anchor. Waves of ecstasy washed through her with each stroke. They moved together, their bodies and breaths in exquisite harmony.

The peaks of pleasure rose and fell between them, mounting bit by bit, burning hotter and brighter with each union. Their breath shortened and their mutual craving intensified. A rushing fever erupted within her, pushing her beyond herself. She gasped, feeling him harden within her cunt, and she exploded into a fiery downpour of delight.

"Beccs," he groaned.

She gripped his neck before licking his ear. "Cum, baby," she said and his hardened body turned to stone, sending her off into bliss again as he exploded within her cunt. They trembled within each other's embrace, clinging to the long awaited reunion.

They recovered and she covered him in adoring soft kisses. Rebecca felt her entire being smile and she looked down into his intense loving gaze. He pushed his hand through her hair and kissed her. He cradled her against him, laying her on the bed beneath him. They caught their breath and he continued to kiss and tease her lips.

"You're feeling better," he said in the relaxed quiet with a smile.

"Because of you," she replied, her hand grazing his cheek and he kissed her nose. "I love you, Eric."

His eyes widened a bit and she wondered if she'd just put her foot in her mouth. Before she could regret anything, he kissed her with a deep tenderness and she felt him relaxing around her.

"I love you, too."

Chapter Fourteen

Six weeks later . . .

"Stiles."

"Detective Stiles, this is Arthur Johnson, Sub Warden of the LVDT."

"What can I do for you, Warden?"

A few weeks after Rebecca's release from the hospital, they both went back to work and life began again. They took it a day at a time. Each of them had crap to deal with and there was a long road ahead. Each morning he woke with her in his arms and he knew he could never be without her.

The first night he'd gone back to work, he returned late and crawled into bed next to her. For the first time, he released all of the frustrations and horror of his day. He snuggled around her warm sleeping body and they faded away into the darkness. He'd never known how much he was dragging with him until he forced himself to let it go. He had to admit it he was delving into new territory. He now had someone to go home to and it changed things.

"I am sorry to bother you but I am required to follow up on all requests."

"I'll do whatever I can to help," Eric replied, regretting answering the phone.

"We have a prisoner here by the name of Jorge Reynolds," the Warden said

Eric motioned to Lug. "What about Reynolds?" Eric asked, feeling anxious.

"He's asking to speak with you."

"Do you know why?"

"We're not sure, but he had a visitor so she may have had something to do with it."

"Who was the visitor?"

"We're not sure, she signed in as an Abigail Lockhart."

Eric wrote the name down on a piece of paper. "Do you have a description?"

"We're bringing up the video feed now, but the guard said she was about 5'5, thin, Caucasian, blue eyes and long thick curly red hair."

Eric stopped writing, the blood draining from his face. "How long ago was she there?"

"About two hours ago," the warden replied. "We aren't sure if it's related, but we wanted to pass on the message."

"Yeah, thanks for the information."

"Anytime, let me know if we can be of any assistance."

"I appreciate it, we will," Eric replied, then hung up the phone.

"What's up?"

"Jorge Reynolds is asking to see me," Eric said, his mouth bone-dry.

Lug reached across, looking at his notes. "Who's Abigail Lockhart?"

"The name of Reynolds's recent visitor."

"Fun."

"Oh no, it gets better."

"What?"

"Apparently she's Rebecca's twin."

A few hours later, he and Adam wound up at Circus-Circus. A deceased cocktail waitress was found by some tourists in the hallway of the 18th floor.

He met his partner beside the body and they started the

investigation. Eric was glad to have something to focus on other than the unsettling request from a psychotic killer. The partners worked well into the early morning hours, interviewing witnesses, looking at the evidence and following up with potential suspects. The night ended in a collar and Eric headed home.

His mind went back to the odd request from Reynolds and his mysterious visitor. The description of the woman matching Rebecca turned in his gut. He pulled up to the house and debated whether he was going to say anything to her about it.

He felt like he should tell her, but he also worried about her unconscious reaction. He'd promised her it was over and he didn't want to frighten her without need. He decided to keep it to himself for now, until he knew what Reynolds was looking to accomplish.

He stepped out of the truck, glancing at his watch, realizing it was late. He reset the alarm before moving through the house and walked into the bedroom. He stripped down, put on a fresh t-shirt and a pair of boxers, then crawled into bed. His arms wrapped around her warmth. She stirred a little and then snuggled into him.

"I missed you."

"I missed you, too," he said, breathing her in while nuzzling her neck.

"What time is it?"

"A little after three, go back to sleep."

"Maybe I don't want to go back to sleep," she said, turning into him.

He leaned down, kissing her, his hand brushing her cheek.

"See, that is much more fun than sleeping."

"Definitely is. However, you have to work in a few hours. I seem to recall something about a quarterly review and a doctor's appointment?"

"You're no fun," she replied with a smirk, kissing him again before snuggling into his chest. He held her close, reveled in her warmth, the events of the day washing away with each breath.

"Hey, what's up?"

"So how did it go?" he asked, not even bothering with a hello.

"Hi to you, too, my day is going great, thanks."

"Beccs."

"He gave me a clean bill of health."

"Did he say anything?"

"No, he ran some tests, took some blood, but said everything looks good."

"Good. So how has your day been?"

"Funny, Stiles."

"Okay seriously, everything is good?"

"Yes, I'm fine. I've been fine for over a month. You can officially stop hovering."

"Well I wouldn't go that far."

"Cute. Okay, I have to go. I have a meeting in ten minutes I'm not prepared for."

"Have fun, love you."

"Love you, too, bye," she replied and her new assistant, Penny, walked into her new office with a stack of files. "Tell me you have the numbers from last night."

"I have the numbers from last night."

"Really?"

"Yes."

"You're a goddess!"

"Well thanks, boss."

Rebecca took the files and began looking at the work on

her desk. She struggled with replacing Mindy, but such was demanded. She started interviewing. Penny was open, honest, bubbly and kind. Rebecca gave her the job and so far, so good.

Her mind drifted back to her conversation with Eric. He was overprotective and adorable. Since her release from the hospital, he'd been wonderful, supportive and amazing. They'd taken it a day at a time and she was astonished at how comfortable it had all been, an ease she wasn't accustomed to. While they were still in the honeymoon phase, she couldn't see anything changing. Even the small disagreements they'd had were swift and finished.

The biggest adjustment she had to make was to his job. He was gone all hours of the night, always on call, but most of all, his job was dangerous. She trusted him to be careful. She knew he was good at what he did, but it offered little relief in the middle of the night when she missed him.

They hadn't talked about it, but he seemed to understand. She noticed him taking the time to text or call her when he was away. When the opportunity arose and he'd been away from her for a while, he would come home to see her or snuggle in bed for a little while. He was trying and that was all she could ask.

Penny motioned it was time for the meeting.

She walked down to the conference room. The only thing left unresolved from the whole horrible situation was Charlie. She hadn't seen him since the day she spoke to him in the hospital. Harry told them he'd taken off for the coast for a while. She felt awful about what happened, but Harry reassured her he would be fine, she just needed to be patient.

The meeting was tedious and boring, just like the three following it. Once finished, she locked herself in her office to plow through her emails. She got halfway through them when her phone rang. "This is Rebecca."

"Good Afternoon, is this Rebecca Gailen?"

"Yes it is, can I help you?"

"Yes, ma'am, I am calling in regards to your credit account with Chase. We are showing it is ninety days past due. We were hoping we could set up a payment with you to bring the account to current."

"Of course. I am so sorry I wasn't aware I had missed a payment. How much is past due?"

"The minimum balance due is three thousand eight hundred and fifty dollars," the man quoted.

"That is the minimum payment?"

"Yes, Ms. Gailen."

"Can you tell me what the full balance is?"

"As of today the balance stands at thirty-three thousand five hundred and sixty dollars."

"I'm sorry, did you just say thirty-three thousand dollars?"

"Yes."

"Okay, I uh . . . can you send me a copy of the bill? I will set up a minimum payment today, but I need a copy of the full bill sent to me, please."

"Of course," he replied and then proceeded to take down her bank information and her email address.

Rebecca hung up the phone, puzzled by the conversation. She sat back in her chair and then saw Penny waving to her for her next meeting.

"What've we got?"

"Three men well-dressed, no ID, but each had over 10K in cash on them."

"That's a lot of money, but not unusual considering," Eric commented, lifting the tarp off one of the bodies and stopped, looking up at Adam. "Are they all like this?"

"Yeah."

"Did you call Davis?"

"Not yet." Eric rose from his crouched position, rubbing the back of his neck. Dead before them were three very high-end dead drug runners. All had been executed at close range, which meant someone was in town, cleaning up. Two more bodies turned up in the next twelve hours. He walked into the station, fourteen hours later in desperate need of sleep, and felt his cell buzzing in his pocket.

Busy night?

Something like that.

You coming home for dinner?

Hopefully.

Donna's making lasagna.

Tease.

Is it working?

Yes.

Love you.

I love you, too.

He plowed through and headed home to find Rebecca in the kitchen, pulling out plates for dinner. He threw down his keys and swept her into his arms, planting a firm kiss on her lips.

"Welcome home."

"I missed you."

"I missed you, too," she replied with a smile, affectionately stroking his cheek.

"When are Donna and the gang due to arrive?" He couldn't resist nibbling on her neck.

"Any minute, so if you want to jump in the shower you should probably go now."

"You're ruining my fun," he complained and she moved out of his embrace and back to the plates.

"Not ruining, just delaying," she replied with a laugh.

He headed to the bedroom, closing the door behind him.

Half an hour later, he stepped back into the kitchen, greeted by the entire crew—Donna, Mike, Jerry, Mac and even Harry. The house was a bustle of noise and activity. With several conversations going on at once, he relaxed next to Rebecca, enjoying the chaos of it.

After dinner, the chatting continued. Eric rose and gathered the plates off the table. He followed Rebecca into the kitchen, making note she hadn't eaten much of her food. He scraped the dish's contents into the garbage and heard his phone ring. Picking it up, he saw Adam's number and answered. "Stiles."

"We need you."

"Okay, I'm on my way." He hung up the phone and Rebecca looked to him, her head tilted.

Ignoring the continued activity around them, he walked to her, taking her face in his hands before kissing her forehead. "I love you."

"I love you too, be safe."

"I will."

Chapter Fifteen

Reynolds's request to see him, albeit an obvious cry for attention, pulled at his conscious. After discussing it at length with both Adam and Lugow, he relented.

The man warranted a visit, if only to make it clear what would happen if he tried to interfere in their lives. Eric requested a meeting with him. He was escorted to a secure room. A few moments later, the door opened and the prisoner walked in. He sat in the chair and was cuffed to the table. The guard nodded to Eric and left.

"Detective Stiles, you got my message."

"Apparently."

"How is Aurora?"

"I'm not here to talk. What do you want?"

"I must tell you, Detective, I'm ashamed to say my earlier statements in regards to my delight in our lovely piece of sunshine were not entirely accurate."

"How so?"

"She was just so captivating. I couldn't resist the temptation. Her fire was too powerful," he said, groaning like a dog in heat. "Well you know, Detective, don't you? You've seen the fire."

"What the hell do you want?"

"She is a flower to be treasured," he replied, looking to him like he was a child. "Our beautiful Aurora."

"She's not our—"

"She is a challenge, isn't she? Strong and vibrant. I so enjoyed our time together—"

"You told her you wanted to hear her scream! You murdered her best friend, you son of a bitch! You drugged her. You terrified and tortured her for months! She is not your sunshine and she is not Aurora!" he raged. "Thank you though, for reminding me why I need to listen to my gut."

"A means to an end."

"Okay, we're done. If this is some pathetic attempt to change your plea to—"

"A necessary evil to protect her!"

"Guard!" Eric yelled, pounding on the door while Reynolds continued to babble.

"It isn't over, you have to build a wall around her before it's too late," the man begged and the heavy door opened.

Eric stepped out, frustrated by the fact he'd even given the man a chance.

"I'm not the only one who needs her!"

Eric shook the conversation out of his mind. It was all nonsense.

An hour later, he was still annoyed by the waste of time and energy. Adam stood waiting for him at his desk.

"How'd it go?" Adam asked. "Anything interesting?"

"Yeah, he's innocent."

It had been a long day and when three o'clock rolled around, she started packing up her computer. Penny entered the office, putting several files on her desk. "These are for tomorrow?"

"Yes, and I'll have the forecast for you as soon as you get here in the morning."

"Great," Rebecca said, packing the files in her bag. "If you need anything, call me on my cell. I'll be available until about seven. Don't stay too late." She and Eric had plans to go see Lucy and she wanted to change before Eric got home.

"Do you need anything before I go?"

"Nope, I think we are good. Have a good night Ms. Gailen."

"Penny, please call me Rebecca," she said, throwing her bag over her shoulder. "You did a great job today. Thanks."

"You're welcome."

"I'll see you in the morning! Bye!"

She walked into the house, dropping her bag on the couch before going back to the bedroom. Lucy had made great progress since her overdose. Dr. Schaffer was optimistic she'd be able to come home in a few weeks.

Rebecca had seen her sister twice since they'd caught her stalker. Lucy's medications were beginning to take effect and Rebecca started to see her sister returning. Her last visit had been a few weeks ago and she'd seen Lucy laugh. It was vibrant and filled her with hope.

She changed into a comfortable pair of jeans and a t-shirt. She tied her sneakers, hearing her phone ring in the next room. Lucy had asked about their mother's locket last time she'd called. She rose to her feet and moved to the dresser when a wave of fog passed over her eyes. She gripped the dresser, taking a breath, and shook it off. Refocusing, she pulled the locket out of her jewelry box and dropped it into her pocket.

She heard her phone beep with a waiting message. She grabbed an apple off the counter and a water from the fridge. She took a bite out of the apple before grabbing her phone. She had a missed call from Eric. She dialed into her voicemail, listened to the message and deleted it with a deep breath. She pushed away the disappointment and annoyance bubbling in her chest and grabbed her purse, apple and water before heading out to the car.

He was working a case and couldn't get away.

It happened.

The problem was Lucy asked her to bring him along so she could meet the man in her sister's life. Rebecca had been comfortable enough with Lucy to tell her a loose version of their relationship. Despite the holes, Lucy's intuitiveness kicked in and she insisted Rebecca bring Eric to their next visit.

She'd figure out a way to explain it away. Lucy would be disappointed, but she would understand.

Damn it, Eric . . .

Calm down, Beccs it's not a big deal. You can talk about it with him when you get home . . .

Two hours later, she checked in with the desk nurse and took a seat. The deafening quiet was unnerving. Dr. Schaffer had made special arrangements with her to visit after hours and the facility was always a little eerie when she arrived. She saw Dr. Schaffer emerge and she ran her fingers through her hair, pushing off the queasy feeling erupting in her stomach. "Dr. Schaffer."

"Good evening, Rebecca. How are you?"

"I am good, thanks."

"That's great. I know Lucy is looking forward to your visit," he said, escorting her to the back area.

"How's she doing?"

"She's doing great, her progress is astounding. I think you'll be really pleased when you see her."

"That's wonderful," Rebecca said with a nod, unable to shake the uneasiness dripping down her back. "Is there anything I need to know?"

"No, just relax and enjoy your time with your sister," he said before his phone rang and he turned with a wave and an easy smile.

Rebecca turned to face the closed door, her gut telling her to call Eric. She pushed it aside, feeling ridiculous. She reached the door and opened it, then walked into the room. A man lay casually in the bed where Lucy should have been. Rebecca stepped back. She took in the two ominous men standing beside him, but didn't hear the fourth man coming up behind her until it was too late.

"Hello, Rebecca, nice to see you again."

Eric scratched the back of his head, finishing the last of the reports on his desk. Well, the last of the ones due tomorrow anyway. It was after eleven and, grabbing his phone, he wondered if Rebecca was home yet. He hadn't heard back from her when he cancelled and figured she might be annoyed with him.

He'd honestly wanted to go with her to see Lucy. When it came time to leave, they were in the middle of interviewing a suspect, which led them to an apartment and a subsequent arrest. He couldn't leave and he hoped once he explained, she'd understand.

He bid the office farewell and headed home for the evening. Eric called her cell to see where she was and her voicemail picked up. It struck him as odd before he remembered the hospital required cell phones be turned off during visitation. She probably forgot to turn it back on when she left.

It happened.

He was hungry and stopped for a burger on the way home. He arrived at the house forty-five minutes later. Her car was missing from the driveway and he went for his cell again, unlocking the door and disarming the alarm.

Voicemail.

"Hey, I'm home and you're not here. Just wanted to make sure you're okay. Call me back, red."

He walked into the kitchen, and unpacked his dinner. He

stood at the counter and ate. He discarded the trash when he was done and headed to the shower. It hadn't been too bad of a day, all things considered. Despite his conversation with Reynolds, they'd made two collars, one on an old case and then a new. He would've liked to have gone with Rebecca, but duty called.

Beneath the hot streams of water, he wondered if he was facing a battle when she got home. His working at all hours had been a challenge in his previous relationships. He wondered how she was going to react to his last minute cancellation of their plans. His gut told him she'd be irritated. They'd talk about it, come to an understanding and it would be fine. However, the doubtful panicked side of him pictured her ranting about how he didn't care about her or her family, feeling like his job was more important than she was, because he wasn't there to go with her.

He played out the scenario, recalling all the arguments, all the instances he'd faced before with previous women in his life. While he tried to put Rebecca's face into their anger fueled emotional rants, he couldn't.

She didn't and wouldn't fit into that particular mold.

It wasn't how she handled things and he took some comfort in knowing without proof he was right.

He stepped out of the shower and changed into a pair of pajama pants, then walked out to the kitchen. The clock on the microwave caught his eye and he realized it was almost one AM. He took a conscious breath. He filled his lungs to the brim before allowing his mind to react.

He dialed her number. He got her voicemail and hung up in frustration. He didn't want to overreact, but his gut was telling him something was wrong. He changed, grabbed his car keys and jumped into the truck.

Eric called into dispatch to see if there had been any wrecks or breakdowns along the route to the rehab hospital.

His buddy at the station checked and came back with nothing. He wasn't sure if it was a good sign or bad.

He was overreacting. She was still with Lucy. He felt like a dumbass and dialed the facility, asking for Dr. Schaffer. Receiving his voicemail, Eric dialed the operator inquiring about Rebecca's visit. He was told she signed in at a little after seven, but hadn't signed out yet.

Eric debated the information for a moment. He realized she was still with Lucy. Although it seemed odd to him they would allow her to stay so late. He also knew Rebecca had some pull with Dr. Schaffer. He was wide-awake, so he continued on his way to the facility to meet Rebecca.

Better late than never . . .

Chapter Sixteen

A wave of nausea swept through her and she turned onto her side. She coughed, struggling to breathe. The iron taste of blood in her mouth turned her stomach and she bit back the bile rising in her throat. The ground beneath her was cold, damp and hard. It felt like concrete and willing her body to move, Rebecca pushed herself into a sitting position. She looked around, blinking away the spots in front of her eyes.

Hello, Rebecca, it's nice to see you again.

She knew his voice before he even looked at her. The same voice haunted all of her dreams and bludgeoned her in her nightmares.

Marco Valnes.

She took in her surroundings and concluded she was in a basement of some kind. Her gaze fell on Lucy and her heart dropped in alarm. Her sister's unconscious body was a few feet away. Rebecca pulled her legs beneath her and rose to her feet. Shaken and unsteady, she moved toward the wall, leaning against the jagged stone.

Breathe, Beccs . . . breathe . . .

Her mind began to clear and she stumbled to Lucy. Rebecca knelt beside her, pulling her sister's head into her lap. She smoothed Lucy's hair away from her face. She wondered where they were and what Marco had planned. The possibilities pushed through her like a dagger, panic bubbling in her chest.

We have to get out of here.

The air was thick and musty, clinging to her lungs. She scanned the room for any kind of light. The only cut in the surrounding gray seemed to be a single bulb in the center of the room. Surrounded by concrete, above her was a ceiling lined with pipes and wooden beams. To her right was a brittle looking staircase with a single door at the top.

Without warning, her emotions rose into her chest. Overwhelming her with fear, panic, hopelessness and regret. She released a shuddered breathe and her entire being cried in agony.

I just want to go home.

Lucy shifted against her and Rebecca wiped away the stray tears. Her sister opened her eyes and she stuffed all the emotions back into the bottom of her chest. She watched Lucy get her bearings and jerk into a sitting position before she spoke. "Lucy, it's okay."

"Beccs," she gasped, breathless, facing her with fear-filled eyes. "Where are we?"

"I don't know," Rebecca rose to her feet and Lucy followed. Her mind shifted and she realized she needed to help Eric find them.

"We need to get out of here, we can't . . ."

"It's going to be okay, we're going to get out of here." She ripped off a piece of her shirt. She pushed her fingers into her hair and tugged out a few strands. She wrapped it around the small piece of cloth and dropped it against the wall where she'd woken.

"How?"

"I don't know, but we'll figure something out." A rattling screech echoed through the room and the door opened. Two men stepped down the stairs followed by Marco. The sisters turned to face their captors and Rebecca stepped in front of Lucy.

He faced them and she waited for him to say something when an explosion erupted against her cheek. She fell back, smacking her head on the concrete.

"*Beccs!*" Lucy screamed.

She tried to recover. Pulled to her feet, her head spun when she felt a hand on her face. He circled her, his breath heating her neck. She struggled to gulp back her revulsion.

"We're going to have fun, you and me," he baited with a heady growl, his arm sliding around her waist, pulling her against him.

"Just let Lucy go and I'll do whatever you want."

"You'll do whatever I want or I'll slit her throat," he growled into her ear, his hand wrapping around her neck. He began to squeeze.

Rebecca tried to stay calm, but as his grip tightened, she started to lose air and panic set in.

"*No! Stop!*" Lucy screamed in protest.

Spots blurring her vision, she clawed at his hands.

"Marco, please stop!"

Marco released his hold and Rebecca fell hard to her knees.

Lucy fell back onto the ground.

Rebecca gasped for air.

Marco loomed. "Where is it?"

"I don't know!"

"Damn it, Lucy. Don't play with me!"

"I'm sorry! I just don't know . . ."

"What . . ." Rebecca started and then began to cough, her chest bellowing in pain. "What's he talking about?"

"Nothing, Beccs, you can't . . . please, Marco, just let us go!"

"It's too late for that."

"What do you mean?"

"Tell me where it is!" Marco growled, grasping Lucy by the arms.

"Let her go!" Rebecca demanded, her legs shaking beneath her. "What is it that you want?"

"The necklace!"

"What necklace?"

"Mom's locket."

"That's what this is about? A goddamned necklace?"

Eric pulled into the parking lot of the Rehab facility. He saw Rebecca's car and pulled in next to it. His keys flipping in his hand, he headed to the main doors. He heard a click. The hairs on the back of his neck rose. Eric moved for his gun. The slice of a gunshot cut through the air, but he had no time to react. A fiery spike ripped at his side, his body crashed onto the ground and there was only blackness.

Agony shot through his limbs. He tried to move, but his body refused to respond. He heard someone call to him and he struggled to lift himself out of the blackness. The voice was familiar, but elusive. He forced his eyes to open. Unable to focus, panic swept through him and his consciousness began to wake.

"Eric, can you hear me?"

"Son, can you hear us?"

Eric opened his eyes again, his brain beginning to cooperate. "Dad?"

"There he is."

"Hey, brother, you scared us," Charlie said.

He tried to push the wavy feeling enveloping him away. "Where am I?"

"You're in the hospital."

"What happened?" Eric fought with his brain, struggling to remember what happened.

"You were shot."

Eric's heart leapt from his chest, his memory slapping him

from behind. "Rebecca."

"Eric, stop . . ."

"Where's Rebecca?"

"Was she with you when this happened?"

"No . . . I mean . . . I went to the hospital when she didn't come home. She was with Lucy," Eric stumbled, not giving his mind any choice but to focus. "Where is she?"

They exchanged hesitant glances, but remained silent.

"Where is she?"

"We . . . we don't know, she's missing," Harry explained.

All of the air in the room disappeared. "What do you mean *she's missing*?"

"They found her car parked outside the hospital next to yours, but there's no trace of her or Lucy," Charlie answered.

"What happened? Someone must know where they went, they couldn't have just disappeared!" he insisted, willing his body to move, but receiving a screaming of agony by his muscles in response.

"Son, you have to calm down, they're doing everything they can to find her—"

"Who's doing everything? I need my phone . . . I need to get out of here!"

"Eric, you're not going anywhere until you calm down!" Henry scolded and pushed him back on the bed.

Eric's body screamed in alarm, his mind racing out of control.

"Now I know you're panicked about the situation, but we need to take this a step at a time. I'm going to get the doctor and we'll talk about what to do next."

His father exited the room. Eric took a breath and his gaze went to Charlie.

"You have to help me get out of here."

"I don't have to help you do anything."

"Charlie, please . . . she's missing," Eric pleaded, his overwhelming emotions getting the better of him. "I can't sit here . . . she's . . . I have to find her."

Charlie walked out the door.

Eric felt like someone sat on his chest and a moment later, his father returned with the doctors. He sat through what seemed to be an endless examination. All the while, the clock in his head ticked away the lost moments he had to find her.

The doctors finished and Eric asked his father to get him something to drink. Eric pulled the tubes and wires from his body, getting out of the bed. He stumbled to the armoire, his left side screaming in protest. He ignored the pain, pulling on his pants and shirt. The door opened and Charlie walked into the room, meeting his brother's eyes. Eric took a breath, not knowing what was going to happen. He was either saved or screwed.

"I parked the truck around back, so we're going to need to take the stairs down. You up for it?"

"Yeah," Eric replied with a nod, studying Charlie's expression. "What do you want to do about Dad?"

"Leave him a note. We'll call him from the road."

Eric took a seat, unable to figure out how he was going to tie his shoes. Charlie unexpectantly crouched down in front of him and tied his shoes.

"I'm not doing this for you. I'm doing this for Rebecca."

"Understood."

"What's going on?"

"Nothing you need to know. All you need to worry about is doing exactly as you're told or little Lucy will suffer the consequences. Do we have an understanding, Ms. Gailen?"

"Yes." She felt Lucy grasp her hand. They rode in silence

and Rebecca's mind spun. She swore she could hear Eric's voice in her head, telling her to just do what they asked. She needed to stall until he could find them. She just needed to keep them in one piece until he arrived with the cavalry.

The truck stopped and Lucy looked at her in apprehension. They sat for a moment. Rebecca looked out the window. There was nothing but blackness. A light flicked on in the distance, revealing a gravel-coated parking lot and Marco shifted.

"Let's go." The thug in the passenger's seat got out of the truck and pulled open Marco's door.

He got out, pulling Lucy along with him, and then motioned for Rebecca to follow.

She slid beyond the door and a heated wind hit her cheek. Marco grumbled something to the thug, who then disappeared. Rebecca saw a dim light coming from the back of the truck. She waited, keeping her eyes steady with Marco's. The thug reappeared, holding a silver briefcase.

He handed it to her and she took it.

"Walk it to the trashcan and wait. A man will arrive. Exchange our briefcase with his and walk away."

Rebecca nodded, glancing at Lucy before she moved. There were no vehicles in sight, only a single light pole next to a trashcan. Suitcase heavy in her hand, she filled her lungs. The cool titanium handle smooth in her palm, she gripped it a little tighter and stepped forward.

Just do the exchange and get out. Simple.

She stopped, the trashcan less than a foot away, and waited. Her gaze scanned the surrounding darkness and found nothing familiar. The crunching of footsteps caused her heart to thud in her ears. The steps came closer. She gulped back the bile rising in her throat.

Breathe. Simple. Breathe.

A gruff well-dressed man appeared from out of the darkness.

Rebecca met his gaze.

He stopped with a small nod.

She adjusted the hand holding the briefcase, her gaze unwavering.

"Ladies first," he said, his voice a pitch higher than she expected.

Unsure what to do, she lifted the case and stepped forward. He mirrored the motion and they grasped the other's case. Rebecca watched his expression and they released their grips. The transfer complete, each was now in possession of the alternate case.

The man nodded and she took a step back before looking to Marco. He waved her return and she started the walk back to the SUV. Her mind racing forward, she pictured how this was going to end. Bristling anger crawled up her back and her gut clenched.

One of Marco's thugs was at the back of the truck. The other was still in the driver's seat, door closed. Marco and Lucy stood alone at the side of the truck. Rebecca heard a phone ring and slowed.

Marco pulled away and his grip on Lucy loosened. He holstered his gun and answered the phone.

Rebecca locked Lucy's eyes. Unable to hesitate, she pulled her arm back and swung the briefcase hard, aimed at Marco's head. It made contact with his throat and he staggered back, stunned.

"*Lucy, run!*" Rebecca kicked him in the face.

He fell back, landing hard on the ground.

She dropped the case and followed her sister's form within the shadows ahead. She heard Marco bellowing orders. She pushed herself to move faster when a crack of lightning exploded behind them. A searing pain knocked her off her feet. She curled into herself before she hit the ground with a thud.

She reeled and tried to recover when a booted foot slammed her in the chest, flipping her onto her back. The air pushed out of her, she curled in pain. Her eyes teared and grayness began to envelope the world.

Her leg throbbed and her stomach cramped. She was yanked to her feet by her hair. Rebecca leaned against unknown arms. Her eyes shifted to Marco's inflamed face and a trickle of blood fell from his mouth.

"She's gone. It's too dark, there's no way to find her."

The voice came from somewhere beyond her vision. Marco growled in frustration and then stomped around like a spoiled child.

She got away.

"What are we missing?"

The large table filled with evidence stared back at them. He knew the answer was there and yet they couldn't see it. Eric, Charlie and Lugow struggled to put the pieces together. They scoured the evidence, hoping to find some clue to where Marco had taken Lucy and Rebecca.

If he was the one who'd taken her, which he didn't know for sure.

Everything that could be done was being done. The problem was they had nothing to go on. They had theories, but no evidence.

Eric had never related to the term *sick with worry*, until now. Since Rebecca's disappearance, he found himself gasping for air, fighting off nausea and wrangling over a flood of overwhelming emotions.

"The connection."

"What?" Eric asked.

"That's what we've been missing, the connection between Reynolds and Rebecca," Lug replied as he entered the room just behind him.

"I thought he was in jail?" Charlie asked.

"He is," Eric replied, his focus on Lug.

"You lost me, what?" Charlie stammered.

"It's what we've been missing all along," Lug continued. "When Rebecca was being stalked, we thought it was Valnes, but we could never connect the two. You caught Reynolds and it was a done deal."

"So?" Eric pushed.

"So, Reynolds's last known residence was Seattle," the man explained with an edge of hope. "We ran his DNA through the national database. Several hits came back, including a partial, from Marco Valnes."

"They're related?" Charlie clarified in confusion.

"Half-brothers, according to the documentation. Same mother, different fathers," Adam explained, joining them.

"He's family," Eric commented in agreement.

"What?" Charlie asked, still confused.

"They're brothers," Eric said, looking to his brother. "Think about it. What if Marco needed to find Lucy, but didn't want anyone to know he was looking for her?"

"He would send someone he could trust would keep it under wraps." Charlie answered.

"And knowing his brother is a psycho, he tells him to look but not touch." Adam added

"Stalking Rebecca wasn't enough," Lug continued. "Reynolds couldn't control himself, so he started killing."

A means to an end. A necessary evil to protect her!

It isn't over, you have to build a wall around her before it's too late . . .

I'm not the only one who needs her . . .

"Keeping his promise, but also fulfilling his own needs," Charlie surmised.

"I went to see Reynolds yesterday. He was babbling, but seemed . . . frantic." Eric reran the encounter in his head.

"So Valnes sends his brother here to watch and or terrorize Rebecca. It could be Reynolds in his own sick way fell for her," Lug offered.

"He was scared . . . he knew this was going to happen and he was trying to warn me."

"Which means he would be willing to help us," Charlie added

"Exactly," Lug confirmed.

"Do you think he knows what Valnes is after?"

"Won't know until we ask."

CHAPTER SEVENTEEN

Her mind heavy, her body began to awaken. Piece by piece, the pain started to pulse through her muscles. It started with the burning ache of her leg and moved up to a spiraling throb in the small of her back, a hardness in her chest and then blinding pain behind her eyes.

She tried to move. At the scrape of metal, her body trembled in resistance. Her eyes opened to faint whispering light and a pipe covered ceiling.

Another basement.

Her mind spun, but she allowed herself to just breathe and not move. She waited for her thoughts to settle.

She got away.

Rebecca opened her eyes again, taking a deep breath of relief. Lucy managed to get away and she prayed her sister was somewhere safe. Now she just needed to keep her head straight until Eric found her, or another opportunity for escape presented itself.

She lifted off the hard ground and her body screamed in protest. Cold metal lay against her hand. She grabbed one of the surrounding pipes, using it to sit upright. The area was much smaller than the previous room, with no break of light except a single door.

Rebecca pulled her throbbing right leg beneath her and noticed an unfamiliar weight around her ankle. The scraping of metal broke through the darkness and she reached down to discover thick rusted metal. Her eyes began to adjust to the lack of light. She focused on the area to see an ancient lead manacle beneath her hand. It was attached to a bulky chain lying heavy on the floor. She followed it along the wall before ending at a set of large solid pipes.

Beautiful.

She stretched out her opposite leg to examine her injury. She pulled at the fabric covering her leg, until she saw blood. It didn't look bad, a simple flesh wound. She debated whether to expend the energy to stand. Before she could decide, the door opened.

Two of Marco's thugs enter the room. They wordlessly unlocked the binding around her leg and hauled her to her feet. Once her leg was free, they yanked her forward and dragged her out of the room. They exited the basement prison and it took a moment for her eyes to adjust before she could discern where she was. An open luxury house. They led her down a hallway, shoved her into a room and locked the door. The room was beautiful. Hardwood floors, cream painted walls, and an antique bed covered in copper hued pillows and blankets.

She moved to the windows and discerned the seal fusing the frames and thick Plexiglas. A second door led to a lush windowless bathroom. Her hand pushed through her hair in frustration. She moved back into the main room. She faced the bed. Its softness called to her weary body. She struggled not to lie down and let herself sink into mindless bliss.

It was then she noticed the black dress lain out on top and a pair of black stilettos on the floor.

"Get cleaned up and put on the dress. You have an hour." The voice echoed through the small room.

"Why should I?"

The door opened. A thug entered, his gun poised against his chest. "You have an hour," the faceless voice repeated.

She begrudgingly grabbed the dress off the bed. The thug's eyes boring into her back, she moved to the bathroom and closed the door.

Shit.

Reluctantly stripping, she stepped into the shower. Unable to take any enjoyment out of the heated streams of water sliding against her body, she effectively washed away the physical dirt. Her skin, however, continued to crawl with the residual filth of discomfort covering her body. Without warning, the world around her went fuzzy. She planted her hands against the tile of the wall, waiting for the spell to pass.

Come on Beccs, you need to pull it together. You can't lose it yet. You have to keep going.

You have to keep going.

You can do this . . . just breathe . . .

The shower allowed her to breathe and her sight cleared. She stepped out and shivered, despite the warmth of the room. The dress slid over her body, but its flawlessness made her feel disjointed and foreign. She tugged at the zipper and took in her reflection, her bruised face staring at her. She gulped back the tears threatening to fall. She acknowledged all the damage he had done and her hands shook as she fought for control.

She ached for Eric. Closing her eyes, she could almost feel his arms around her, the warmth of his chest against her cheek.

He will come.

He will find me.

She heard the door of the bedroom opening and spun toward it. The bathroom door opened. She saw Marco, who motioned her to join him. She lingered, looked at the armed guard behind him and then moved.

"Rebecca, you have to admit. I have extremely good taste." He moved around her, licking his lips while scrutinizing her body. He moved closer.

She restrained her disgust with a short breath.

"Your body really does fill that dress in all the right

places."

She felt him just behind her shoulder. His hand rested on the small of her back. It proceeded to shift down her hip and then across her lower abdomen like a tentacle. He moved to face her, his eyes cold and darting. He decided to brush the inside of her leg and she suppressed a tremble of loathing.

"It's not often a dress pales in comparison to the body it encompasses. It's too bad Detective Stiles isn't here to enjoy it with me."

His breath hit her neck, a chill ran up her spine, the blood draining from her cheeks.

"You look so pale, sweetheart, did I hit a nerve?"

Mid-breath, she straightened her back and lowered her shoulders. His face stopped within inches of hers.

"What you did with Lucy was . . . brave," he taunted, staring down at her lips. "It makes me wonder about Detective Stiles's bravery in his time of trial."

"What are you boasting about now?" Her voice with thick sarcasm, she lifted her chin in defiance of him.

"Tit for tat, Beccs." His hand rested on her hip and he smiled. "You take something from me and I take something from you. You didn't really think I was going to let it go . . . did you?"

Her heart panicked uncontrolled, but she refused to take what he was saying at face value. He was taunting her, trying to get her to fight him so he had an excuse. He was pissed at what she'd done so he was trying to torture her.

His eyes remained focused on her lips. She turned her face away from him in disgust. Within a breath, he yanked at her hair and she felt his tongue against her now exposed neck.

"You don't believe me?"

She fought the rising fury sweeping through her.

Marco held a cell phone up for her to see. A picture of Eric on the ground covered in blood filled the small screen, his face dark, his eyes closed.

She turned away in an attempt to deny the panic rising in her chest. His grip on her hair tightened, forcing her to look at the image. Despite her efforts to push it out of her mind, her body trembled when the reality hit.

"He's not coming for you, Rebecca. You're all alone. No one is coming for you, and soon, you won't want them to."

Eric took a deep breath, not knowing if he was prepared for the task at hand. He was going to have to ask for help from the man who still haunted her dreams. He pushed the residual rage down into the bottom of his stomach and focused on what they needed to know.

"You know how this has to go."

"Yeah."

"Okay."

Eric took another breath before the door opened and then followed Lugow into the room. He was too close to the situation. So he agreed to let Lug handle the interrogation while he watched from the sidelines.

Reynolds's gaze attached to him and Eric ignored the hair rising on the back of his neck. He shoved his hands in his pockets, taking his position against the back wall.

"It's so nice to see you again, Detective Stiles," Reynolds greeted.

Eric gulped back the bile rising in his throat.

"Mr. Reynolds, I expected to see your counsel in attendance," Lug said.

"There's no need, I have nothing to hide."

"So, Jorge, what can you tell me about Marco Valnes?"

Eric watched the man's body straighten. He lifted his hands from beneath the table and flattened them on its surface.

"We know Marco Valnes is your brother. We know he sent you here to watch Rebecca and Lucy Gailen." Reynolds's gaze move to Eric. "I need to know why."

"He needed me," Reynolds replied, an affectionate smile edging his lips. "My brother needed my help."

"What did he ask you to do, exactly?"

"Keep an eye on things. Special things."

"What special things?" Lug asked.

Reynolds's eyes shined. "Lucy, a masterpiece, waiting to behold. They all wanted her, that's why she's locked away."

"So, Lucy Gailen," Lug said, filling in the cracks. "What about Rebecca? Did your brother tell you anything about her?"

"Aurora," Reynolds replied, his hands going back beneath the table.

"Did he have any special instructions for you in regards to Rebecca?"

Reynolds shifted in his chair, his gaze darting around the room.

"Jorge, you liked Rebecca, didn't you? You came here to protect Lucy. You saw Rebecca and you were taken with her."

"Sunshine," he said with a shuddered breath. His hands rose onto the table again, lying flat against its surface. "So exquisite, invigorating, hair like the rising sun, eyes like the rolling sea. Watching her was like watching a proud lioness. Her strength and defiance is intoxicating."

"Marco said you couldn't have her, didn't he?"

Reynolds fingers clawed into the table.

Eric's stomach began to knot.

"You had to stay away from her, didn't you, Jorge?"

"I had one. I think you'll remember her, Eric. She was the closest I ever came," he said, looking to him in satisfaction.

"But she lied. It was fake. Her lovely locks were fake. I should have known, but I was always a sucker . . ."

"Jorge, what does Marco want with Rebecca?"

"Nothing."

"Jorge . . ."

"It's over."

"What's over?"

"It doesn't matter. It's too late. All that matters is that she'll remember. She'll always remember . . ." Reynolds said, looking to Eric in perverse confidence. "She's hasn't forgotten me, has she, Detective? She still sees me waiting for her there in the shadows, breathing on her beautiful ivory neck."

Eric forced himself to not react to the man's fixation, demanding his body ignore the bubbling rage threatening to suffocate him.

"Tell me why he came here, Jorge," Lug asked, appealing to his affection for Rebecca. "Tell me what Marco came for so we can find him and bring Rebecca back."

"I forgot to ask the last time we met. How long was it until your brother figured it out?" Reynolds asked. "In watching her, it was almost impossible not to observe you as well. It must've been agonizing to keep yourself away from such an incredible creature. Your strength of will and loyalty to your brother is to be commended, if not so short lived."

"What does Marco want, Jorge?" Lug asked in an attempt to retake control.

"If you think about it, you should be thanking me, Detective Stiles. If it wasn't for me, you would've never realized just how much you love her."

"Why has he taken them?" Lug interjected.

"You would've walked away and never known her sweet breath or exotic smile. The way she curves under your hand when you touch her or the smell of her hair as it brushes your cheek.

"What is he after?" Lug asked, his voice steadily rising.

"How it feels to be completely loved."

Eric found himself gasping for air.

"*Enough!*" Lug demanded, slamming his fists down on the table. "What does Marco want?"

"I have a request."

"What?"

"I want Detective Stiles to say thank you," Reynolds said, his eyes challenging. "And I want him to answer two questions, truthfully."

The request was simple enough and yet Eric felt shocked and struggled against it. How was he supposed to thank the man who hunted and tortured the woman he loved? And what questions? "Why?" Eric asked, his gaze locking Reynolds's.

"Think of it as a test."

"I don't do games."

"It's two words and two questions."

"And if I agree?"

"I'll tell you what Marco is looking for and possibly where to find him."

"Possibly?"

"Nothing is for certain, Detective. He's my brother, but I'm not his keeper. I'll give you my best guess."

Eric took a breath, his heart thudding hard against his chest suppressing the oxygen he needed to think. "Fine," Eric agreed, walking to the table. He stopped, laid his hands on the table and met Reynolds's eyes in confidence. "Thank you."

The man took in the response and a regretful smile spread across his face.

"Tell us."

"I still have two questions."

"You tell me what he's after. Then you'll get your

questions."

"The locket. That's what they're all after."

"What?"

"There is a chip hidden in Abigail Gailen's locket. I never found out what was on it. It is apparently of some value to someone," Reynolds explained, his eyes shining. "He's going to sell it to the highest bidder."

"Where?"

"I still have my questions," Reynolds interjected.

Eric held his breath. "Fine, what?"

Jorge threaded his fingers on the table and leaned closer to him. "When your fingertips slide over her skin, is it . . ." the man paused, his eyes closing just before a wanting breath pushed out of his chest. "Unbelievably soft?"

Eric wasn't expecting the simple intimacy of the question. He pushed away from the table, gulping back his torment, his chest stiff and heavy. The monster evoking such revulsion sat patiently waiting for his answer. His eyes opened, looking like a lizard tracking a cricket, he licked his lips. Eric pulled air into his lungs.

Whatever it takes . . .

"Yes," Eric answered, cringing at the man's lustful satisfaction at his response.

"Is she tight?"

Eric's control snapped. His body humming with rage, he hurled the table, slamming Reynolds in the shoulders. The force rocked the chair and it fell back. Eric enjoyed the sound Reynolds's body made when he bounced off the concrete floor.

"Stiles!" Lug warned.

Eric proceeded to place a heavy foot on Reynolds's chest. "I've had enough of your sociopathic horseshit! Tell us what you know! Where is he?"

"You haven't answered the second question, Detective," Reynolds taunted through gasping breaths.

"Please . . . please push me some more," Eric growled, his foot pressing harder against Reynolds's chest and the man began to laugh. "Let some more disgusting descriptions or deranged fantasies fall out of your mouth, so I don't have to wait to kill you!"

"This is a thrill!" Jorge taunted before he met Eric's challenging stare. "He has a house outside Pahrump, off of Rt. 160. If they're still alive, he would hold them there until . . ."

"Until?"

"Until he doesn't need them anymore."

Eric released him and walked to the door.

"Detective."

Eric stopped, but refused to turn.

"Be aware. The devil's face isn't always the ugliest."

Two of his thugs led her to the opposite end of the house. Rebecca took a small breath just before her heel twisted and she fell against the guard on her right. He shifted and caught her before she went down. She kept his eyes for a moment, but then struggled against him in disgust. He raised her back to her feet and she shifted her dress before they started to move again. They walked about another twenty feet until they stopped. One of the guards opened a door and led her inside.

The room was an oversized game room filled with electronics. She heard the door close behind her and she spun to make sure she was alone. Her movement was discreet despite the lack of evident presence in the room. She looked for a place to work.

Lucy is safe.

Eric is gone.

The image of him fallen and bleeding clung to her. It hardened her heart and ripped at her soul with unrelenting teeth, stirring her resolve instead of breaking it. She may be dying inside, but she'd be damned if she would let Marco walk away without reprieve.

Her eyes focused on a vase in the corner of the room. She kept her peripheral view in line with the door. She released the phone from the back of her dress. She had managed to palm it from the guard. Her distraction had worked. The thug was preoccupied with her sudden weakness and she slipped it beneath the back of her bra.

She would need to send JJ Abrahams a note of thanks if she survived.

Her heart pounding, she switched the phone to silent. Without warning, a splintering pain shot through her abdomen. She gasped in surprise, clutching her stomach. She leaned heavily on the table, coping with the sudden but excruciating pain. She focused and dialed 911. Rebecca waited for the faint sound of an operator, before she pushed three numbers consecutively.

Seven-Six-Seven.

She heard voices approaching the door. She dialed it again before dropping it inside the vase, leaving the line open.

The door opened and she straightened her back. A hand wrapped around the base of her neck. She suppressed her reaction, knowing it was Marco. The clenched hand turned her around and she looked at him with a glare.

"Find something of interest?"

"No, just a bunch of garbage. I'm sorry, was I supposed to be impressed?"

His hand tightened around her and the door opened again. Marco's hand moved from her neck to her arm where he cuffed her hands together behind her back.

"What the hell are you doing?"

"You didn't think I got you all dressed up for nothing? You have a visitor."

"What?"

A distinguished olive-skinned man entered the room. He had shoulder length gray hair pulled taut at the back of his neck. Well dressed in a black silk suit and mid-collared European shirt, his dark almost black eyes undressed her while he moved into the room.

His hands in his pockets, the stoic man stopped just inches away from her. His spiced breath assaulted her air. She struggled to breathe and fought to remain in control, despite the tightening in her throat.

The mystery man looked to Marco, who responded by tightening his hold on her arms. The grotesque man approached her and leaned forward, his hands grasping her hips. She tried to move away, but Marco's hold was firm. He pulled her against him and she fought back. The movement seemed to entice him more, his hands moving from her hips up her ribs.

His mouth attached itself to the nape of her neck. She cringed in revulsion, his rancid breath curling against her. She struggled to hold back angry tears. Her body trembled when his hands continued to move upward. His palms covered her breasts and she revolted, fighting harder against Marco's restraint. She felt the zipper of her dress sliding down. She screamed, thrusting her knee into his groin.

"Bitch," Marco said.

Her victim lurched forward in agony. Marco yanked her by the hair. She struggled against him, but his grip remained firm.

The nameless man recovered and eyed her in amusement. Marco held her still as he moved closer. His hand openly groped the exposed skin just below her neck. His hand trailed down, palming her breast again.

"Get away from me, you slug," she spat.

He chuckled. "There's a fire in you." His thick accent rolling over the words, his hand continued to grope her.

"You're alive with passion. Fight all you want, my dear. You're mine now."

CHAPTER EIGHTEEN

Charlie was bringing the car around when Eric's phone rang. "Detective Stiles."

"Detective Eric Stiles?"

"Yes, who's this?"

"Eric, it is Dr. Raines," he heard on the other end and exhaled a deep breath.

"Dr. Raines, it is great to hear from you, but this isn't the best time. Can I—"

"Is it true?"

Eric's heart thudded loudly against his chest.

"When I couldn't reach Rebecca I called Ms. Martin and she told me—"

"Yes, it's true."

"I am very sorry to hear that," the man said in a low voice. "Considering the situation I think—"

"Doc, I appreciate you—"

"Eric, there's something I need to tell you."

It had covered her like a blanket. The lovely warmth had once encompassed her, its comfort sinking into her body and then her soul. It had vanished, into the concrete beneath her cheek and she ached for him. All she could see was his broken bloodied body lying in the street.

Eric . . .

Lurching pain accompanied the reality, effectively pummeling her balanced defenses. The hovering vulnerability crashed down, overtaking her strength. Her weakened body trembled as it besieged and isolated her. The hollow in her stomach bellowed and tensed. It shattered her walls in the form of desperate, fear-filled sobs. They tore through her with an unrelenting force. It magnified her exhaustion while simultaneously extinguishing the little fire that remained.

She huddled within herself, inviting the darkness to caress her weary mind. She waited for it to pull her away, pleading the emptiness for relief. She wanted to let go, to break, and admit her defeat.

About the Author

Amy is a wife, mother of three and full time corporate employee. Amy has two dogs and a cat, enjoys movies, music and spending time with friends. Amy's writing heart beats to the fast paced, twisting, romantic thriller, but has also dabbled in theatre as an actress and director, written young adult romance and actively explored alternative venues for corporate marketing.

Amy works for a global document solutions company and current resides in Texas.

My Mantra

I believe Everything Happens for a Reason

I believe in True Love

I believe in Fate

I believe in Optimism

I believe in Imagination

I believe in Hard Work

I believe in Family

www.ingramcontent.com/pod-product-compliance
Lightning Source LLC
Chambersburg PA
CBHW061515050726
47593CB00002B/575